The London Murder Mysteries

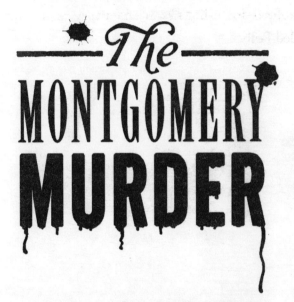

The MONTGOMERY MURDER

CORA HARRISON

PICCADILLY PRESS • LONDON

First published in Great Britain in 2010
by Piccadilly Press Ltd,
5 Castle Road, London NW1 8PR
www.piccadillypress.co.uk

A catalogue record for this book is available
from the British Library

ISBN: 978 1 84812 064 8 (paperback)

1 3 5 7 9 10 8 6 4 2

Printed in the UK by CPI Bookmarque, Croydon, CR0 4TD
Cover design by Patrick Knowles
Cover illustration by Chris King
Cultural adviser: Jaspal S Grewal

*For Noah, Peter, Abe, Alexander, Joel
and Reuben, grandsons of my very dear friends,
Patricia and Doug Hawkes.*

*Special thanks go to Peter who read and
commented on an early draft.*

CHAPTER 1

ALFIE'S GANG

It was a foggy evening in late November. The gas lamps shone like misty balls of light and the horses slipped on the wet streets. Well-dressed Londoners wrapped mufflers over noses and mouths as they rushed home to supper in their warm houses. And four ragged boys, followed by a large dog, emerged from a filthy cellar below the pavement.

The plan had been made . . .

* * *

Alfie grinned and the tight knot of fear in his stomach relaxed – Mutsy always made him laugh. His brother Sammy had just hit the high note of the song and the big, hairy dog joined in immediately, sitting on his back legs with his two front paws in the begging position, his nose lifted towards the sky and howling like a high-pitched fiddle. A crowd was beginning to gather – it always did when Sammy and Mutsy sang.

On this dark and murky evening, Alfie was relying on dog and boy being the focus of all attention. He had set everything up very carefully. Sammy, with Mutsy beside him, was standing on the corner just outside the Covent Garden Theatre, while Alfie himself was about a hundred yards away. Jack and Tom, their two cousins, were also in place.

'He's blind, poor little boy,' said a woman's voice, and Alfie heard the chink of pennies into the tin plate at Sammy's feet. Now was the moment to put his plan into action. The shoppers were gathered around Sammy and Mutsy; nobody would be looking at Alfie.

And then he had a piece of good luck – there was

a loud pop and a hissing sound, and a smell of gas floated down on the fog. One of the gas lamps had gone out. Great! Slowly and quietly, Alfie moved until he was underneath that lamp-post. This would be a good place to lurk unseen. The lamplighter had already shouldered his ladder and gone home, so the corner between Bow Street and Russell Street would now stay dark till morning.

Alfie's stomach was already empty, but it tightened even more with tension. This was his plan and he was the gang leader. It had to succeed. He licked his lips as he glanced around. Jack, his twelve-year-old cousin, was in his place, across the road, just ready to grab the horse's head. Eleven-year-old Tom, Jack's brother, was almost invisible, lurking in the shadowed door-way of a watchmaker. He would have his peashooter ready. Alfie could rely on him. Tom and Jack both had steady nerves and Tom never missed a shot.

Now! The moment they were waiting for! The horse-drawn van turned from Russell Street into Bow Street and a mouth-watering smell of newly baked bread floated above the sour, coal-smoke stench of the fog. Alfie braced himself. He saw the horse rear and kick – Tom had done his task with the peashooter. Alfie didn't even look towards Jack – his cousin could always handle horses. Instantly he dashed to the back of the van.

It was all working. He could hear Jack's voice shouting, 'It's all right, Mister, I've a hold of him.' Now Alfie had his hand in the back of the van. The loaf was so soft and warm he could almost taste it. Tom was coming towards him. Between them, with luck, they would be able to snatch enough bread to last them for the next few days. No alarm was shouted; the crowd continued to listen as Sammy broke into his comic song, 'The Catsmeat Man'.

Suddenly Alfie felt an arm around his neck, throttling him. He dropped the loaf and wheeled around to see a navy-blue uniform with the number twenty-two on the collar.

A gruff voice said, 'You come along with me, lad.'

The cops had nabbed him.

CHAPTER 2

THE DEAD BODY

Alfie did not struggle. There was no point. The policeman had a firm grip of one arm now and was dragging him along the street. He tried a gentle wriggle – perhaps he could leave his jacket behind – but it was no good. Alfie knew where they were going. The Bow Street Police Station was next door to Bow Street Magistrates' Court. He would probably be in front of the bench in less than half an hour.

What would be the sentence? Most likely, three months' hard labour – that was the usual. He had never been in prison himself, but he knew many boys who had. Hard labour meant breaking stones, running on the treadmill or sewing mailbags for twelve hours of the day, and no one was allowed to say a word to any other prisoner. That was the worst of all, one boy had told Alfie.

And what would happen to Sammy, his blind brother, and to their two cousins who shared their cellar? Without Alfie, they might all starve. He was the one who organised everything, who had seen the comic possibilities in Mutsy with his large paws and his fringe hanging over his eyes, and the one who, until this moment, had kept them all out of trouble.

'In you go.' The blue light outside Bow Street Police Station gleamed through the fog. 'Bet you've stolen that muffler, you little thief.' The constable jerked at the scarf around his neck. 'And that waistcoat, too!' By now they were inside and Alfie was pushed into an office. His bare feet felt the smoothness of the tiled floor.

Carefully he removed his cap and smoothed down his dark curls. *'It doesn't matter about looking poor and having ragged trousers as long as you are polite.'* It seemed like yesterday that his mother had said that, but she had been dead for two years.

The police station was a small, one-storey building. There was an outer room, where three constables stood at tall desks and made notes in books, and an inner room beyond a green painted door. A man with a newspaper came out of that door and immediately PC 22 grabbed Alfie by the arm and hauled him into the back room, giving a quick knock on the still-open door. Alfie felt his legs go weak. He would soon know the worst.

'Caught stealing a loaf of bread from the evening delivery van, Inspector. Make a bow to Inspector Denham, you young ruffian. Shall I take him into the court? The magistrates are still sitting.'

'Yes,' said the inspector absent-mindedly. He was studying some papers on his desk, turning them over and knitting his dark bushy eyebrows over them. Then he waved his hand. 'No!' he said abruptly. 'Just leave him with me, Constable, will you.'

What did he want, wondered Alfie, looking at the inspector as the door closed behind the constable. He was a small man to be in charge of all of these burly constables who could be seen every day, patrolling Bow Street and Covent Garden. He was quick and decisive, though! He looked briefly down each piece of paper, before putting it into one of three neat piles on the desk and going on to the next.

The room was cold in spite of the coal fire burning in a small metal grate. Alfie's sharp eyes noticed that one of the sash cords was broken and the window was sagging down on one side, allowing the damp, freezing air to seep into the little room. He stayed very still, looking attentively at the inspector as he shuffled his papers. When he looked up, Alfie saw that he had a pair of keen eyes, as black as Alfie's own.

'Live around here, do you?' The inspector's tone was casual.

'That's right.' Alfie wasn't going to give any of his gang away.

'Know the St Giles district?'

Alfie nodded. This was unexpected, but welcome. St Giles, a district of tumbledown wood-built houses, where a single room could house up to four families, was a good five-minute walk from Alfie's cellar on Bow Street itself.

'Come with me.' Inspector Denham was on his feet. He opened a door at the back of the office and led the way down a long, dimly lit corridor. There was a damp coldness in the air and a strange smell.

'In here.' Inspector Denham took a large key from the bunch at his waist and opened a door. The room was almost in darkness; there was just one small, high window. It showed as a pale rectangle on the wall, but gave little light. Inspector Denham clanged the door shut behind them and walked confidently forward. Alfie followed him, his heart thumping.

'Ah, that's better.' There was a hiss and a sudden smell of gas, the noise of a match striking, and then the flame sprang up. Alfie took a step backwards, then recovered himself and stepped forward again.

The room was a small one, but it had three occupants. All were lying on high narrow iron beds, covered by a sheet. All were very still. Alfie sniffed the air and knew that the smell was death. He had smelled it often enough. He swallowed once and felt the sweat break out on the palms of his hands.

Why had the inspector brought him in here with these dead men?

CHAPTER 3

GARROTTED!

Inspector Denham went swiftly to the bed at the far side of the room and turned back the top of the sheet from the face.

Alfie took in a long breath as quietly as he could. 'I know him,' he said, trying to sound indifferent. 'I've seen him before.' He examined the purple, swollen face with its faded ginger moustache and sideburns.

'Know his name?'

'Mr Montgomery . . . Mr Montgomery from Bedford Square. Up Bloomsbury way.' Alfie went a little nearer. He had been shocked at first to see a man that he knew, but he had recovered now. He had seen quite a lot of dead bodies in his lifetime.

'When did you see him last?' Inspector Denham was standing in front of the body, slightly blocking Alfie's view.

'Last night in Monmouth Street.'

'Alone?'

'No, he had a girl with him.' Alfie winked, trying to look like a man of the world. He wanted to impress this inspector.

'What's the girl's name?' The question came quickly.

'Don't know.' He did know, but Alfie didn't think that he was going to tell it to Inspector Denham. Betty couldn't have murdered this fellow – he wasn't a very big man, but he was at least twice her weight. Alfie was sorry that he had mentioned a girl now, but no doubt the inspector already knew about this. Alfie edged a bit nearer to the body.

'Been garrotted,' he said. Might as well show the

12

inspector that he wasn't stupid. 'Look at the mark of the wire, there under the chin.'

'I had noticed,' said Inspector Denham dryly. 'We found him in Monmouth Street early this morning.' He leaned over the man and pulled the sheet down the whole way. The body was still dressed: expensive frock coat, colourful waistcoat and over them both a greatcoat of heavy dark wool; check trousers and polished boots finished the outfit. A heavy walking stick was lying beside him. The pockets of the greatcoat were pulled out and protruded at right angles from the body, the clean white linings showing up brightly under the flaring gas lamp.

'Robbed, as you see.' Inspector Denham's voice was neutral.

'Nah.' Alfie gave him a quick grin. He was beginning to understand this policeman. He was testing Alfie. 'Never.'

'Oh? Why not?' There was still no trace of expression in the policeman's voice.

'Why not?' Alfie decided to play along, though he guessed that the inspector knew the truth as well as he did; the man didn't look stupid. 'Why take the stuff from his greatcoat pockets and leave the watch? I can see the chain. It's still on him. Can I touch him?'

'Just the clothes.'

Alfie leaned over and, with the sensitive fingers of an accomplished pickpocket, he pulled out a heavy gold watch from below the man's waistcoat.

'There you are,' he said. He stroked the rounded sides of the gold case, then turned it over and looked with interest at the marks on the back. 'In his fob pocket, the usual place. Any thief would look there first. This is a good watch. He was quite a swell, always.'

'Perhaps the thief forgot about the watch,' suggested Inspector Denham with an expressionless face. 'Out of sight, out of mind, they say.'

'Nah! Never! In any case, why leave the boots? They were in sight. Why not pull them off and take them? I know plenty on Monmouth Street that would give me —' Alfie suddenly remembered that he was talking to an officer of the law, 'at least . . . I've heard that you can get a good price for a pair of boots like that. Nah, this were no thief; this were a toff that garrotted him and then wanted to pretend that he did it just to rob him. I'd lay a bet that Mr Montgomery had nothing at all in those greatcoat pockets. Most of the gents these days keep their money in their trousers or waistcoat pockets. It's obvious to anyone that this were no thief that done this,' he finished.

The inspector said nothing, but Alfie could see an expression of satisfaction on his face. He searched his mind for more memories of Mr Montgomery. The man had returned from India a few months before and Alfie had taken a great interest in the stories about him that Sarah, the scullery maid in the Montgomery house, had told the boys. But would it be safe to talk about these to the inspector?

'What about the ring?' Alfie asked suddenly. 'He always wore a great big diamond ring. I've seen it flashing.'

One hand was half-tucked under the body; ignoring the inspector's order, Alfie reached across and pulled it out. The ring was still there.

'It's embedded in his flesh. He'd put on a lot of weight since he first had that ring,' the inspector said indifferently, watching Alfie closely.

'Most people that I know – most thieves that I've

heard of, would have taken finger and all to get a ring like that,' said Alfie firmly. 'It would be worth a lot, that ring, wouldn't it?'

'I'd say so.' The inspector sounded almost friendly.

Alfie said no more, though, and Inspector Denham, having turned out the gaslight, ushered him through the door and locked it firmly behind them. Even when they were back in the office again, Alfie still kept silent, his mind busily working. What was the inspector up to?

CHAPTER 4

A JOB FOR ALFIE

'What do you know about Mr Montgomery and his household?' It had taken a few minutes for Inspector Denham to make up his mind, but now his tone was sharp, and somehow different.

Alfie sat up a little straighter and assumed a business-like air. He had been about to deny knowing anything more about the dead man, but then changed his mind. It occurred to him that he had passed some sort of trial in there, in that room where the police kept their dead bodies, and he was anxious to retain Inspector Denham's good opinion.

'There's him and his missus, and his son who's a young toff – doesn't do no work, I've heard – and they've got a butler, a coachman, a cook, a house-keeper, a parlour maid and a scullery maid – and some other servants, I suppose.'

'How do you know all this?'

Alfie hesitated. Sarah often fed him on the left-overs from the Montgomery meals and he didn't want to betray her, but after a quick glance at Inspector Denham he changed his mind. The inspector, he reckoned, might be willing to forget about the bread van if Alfie was able to assist him.

Alfie and his gang had known Sarah for about six months now. After hearing his brother Sammy singing in the streets, Mrs Montgomery had got her coachman to bring him to the house at Bedford Square, where she had played the piano while Sammy sang some of his songs. Afterwards, Sarah had been told by the parlour maid to escort Sammy home. She had stayed for half an hour in their cellar, entertaining them all with her stories of the Montgomery household and Mr Montgomery, and how he had been in India for years while his wife, who didn't like India, lived with their son in London. Since then, Sarah had visited the cellar every time she was allowed out to go to night classes or in her free time.

'I know the scullery maid.' Alfie had made up his mind that there could be no harm in admitting that.

'Good.' There was no mistaking the satisfaction in the man's voice, and Alfie began to feel quite interested.

'Do you know anything about Mr Montgomery's earlier life?' the inspector continued.

'He'd been out in India until six months ago, and that's where he made all his money. His missus and his son lived here in London all the time that he was away,' said Alfie.

The inspector nodded. 'That's right and that's where you come in. The son, Mr Denis Montgomery, thinks that his father has been murdered because of something that happened in India. It appears that when Mr Montgomery was out there, a native Indian, working on the tea plantation owned by him and his partner, Mr Scott, was found guilty of stealing a bag of coins and was hanged.'

Alfie shrugged his shoulders; these things happened all the time. In London, when his grandfather was young, they used to hang anyone who stole goods over the value of a shilling. Why should India be any different?

'Now, the butler at the Montgomery household says that he saw a young Indian, not much more than a boy, hanging around their house yesterday. He told Mr Denis about that. It's possible that the hanged man's son came to seek his revenge. There are two ships from the East India Company in dock at the moment, just down river from here.'

'And you want me to sniff around and see if I can come across any sign of this Indian, that right?'

'And anything else that you can find out. Anything about the household – the servants, I mean. Also, anything that passers-by might have seen, either in Bedford Square or in Monmouth Street.'

So that was what Inspector Denham had been after.

'What's in it for me?' It was always worth asking, Alfie thought.

'Perhaps, if you're lucky, the constable might forget what is written down in his notebook about this evening's incident with the bread delivery van.'

Alfie brushed that aside. 'Any reward?' he asked. Although he couldn't read, he had a sharp eye for figures, and the wall outside Bow Street Police Station was papered with posters offering rewards.

'There is a reward of one hundred pounds put forward by Denis Montgomery,' said Inspector Denham cautiously. 'It might be that you could earn yourself some small share in that. Here's a shilling for you in the meantime.' He got briskly to his feet and opened a second door at the back of the room. 'You can go out this way, unless you want to see the constable again.' There was a suspicion of a wink as Alfie walked past, and then the door slammed shut behind him.

Alfie felt quite dazed and for a moment he hardly knew where he was. Then he realised that he was in Crown Court, a small, square, empty space between the police station and the magistrates' court. He gave a quick glance over his shoulder and then ran as fast as he could. He didn't want to linger; he'd had a narrow escape and the sooner he was away from there, the better.

Out in crowded Bow Street, Jack was carefully sweeping horse-droppings from the roadway so that a stout, middle-aged lady could cross. Alfie stood and watched him while his heart slowed down. Jack and Tom's mother had died when Tom was born and Alfie's mother had taken in her sister's two children. No one knew where their father was. On the whole, the cousins got on well. Jack was easy-going and good-natured and always willing for Alfie to be the boss, and Tom, though he could at times be moody and resentful of Alfie's authority, could usually be persuaded by Jack to do what Alfie wanted.

Despite Jack's efforts with the broom, the woman was holding her purple dress high above her ankles, showing a frill of white petticoat. The road was even dirtier than usual because of the fog that had lasted three days already. Alfie noticed that the woman was carrying her basket securely tucked under her shawl, away from the reach of the pickpockets who did such a good trade around the Covent Garden fruit and vegetable market. Her mouth was tight with distrust as she glanced around.

Alfie stood well back from her while she stepped on to the pavement, dropping something into Jack's hand and then hurrying down the street.

'You got out, then.' Jack sounded off-hand, but Alfie could detect a note of relief in his cousin's voice and there was a grin on his freckled face.

'How much did she give you?' Alfie did not want to talk about Inspector Denham out in the street.

Jack opened his hand. 'A farthing,' he said with disgust. 'I thought it would be a halfpenny at least. The old —'

'Look.' Alfie, a smile widening his mouth, gave a nod towards the woman.

A one-horse gig, driven at high speed down Bow Street, had sent a spray of semi-liquid horse dung all over the woman's skirt, even neatly landing a fair-sized dollop on the very crown of her stiff-brimmed bonnet.

Alfie and Jack clutched each other, shaking with merriment at the sight of the woman's disgusted face as she scrubbed at her skirts with a small handkerchief. It felt so good to laugh again after the worries and tension of the past hour that they went on for several minutes.

'Come on,' said Alfie, still chuckling with mirth. He threw his arm over Jack's shoulders, eyeing the brightly lit butcher's shop across the road. 'Let's get some sausages and a loaf of bread. I've got a shilling.'

At that moment, a carriage drawn by four lively horses swung around the corner from Long Acre into Bow Street. The oil lamp, dangling from the back of its roof, flared suddenly, lighting up the shadowy doorway of the house across the road.

Brown-skinned and dressed in dark clothes, his white turban grey with the London dirt, the young boy lurking there had remained invisible up to that moment against the murky wooden door. Now he was sharply illuminated, staring across the road at the two boys. It was unusual to see an Indian in the West End of London and Alfie had no doubt that this must be the boy that the inspector had been speaking of – the boy under suspicion for the murder of Mr Montgomery.

How long had the Indian been standing there, his fist clutched over something hidden? Had he seen Alfie come out of the police station? Did he guess the inspector's commission?

Alfie swallowed twice, almost feeling the bite of a garrotting wire around his throat.

CHAPTER 5

MIXED UP WITH MURDER

'Get down, Mutsy, get down, you old slob!' Alfie wrestled with the dog at the door to the stairs leading down to the cellar where the four boys lived.

The cellar had been the home of Alfie's parents before they died, and the first thing Alfie thought of every Saturday, after he had paid the rent-collector, was how to get money for the next week's rent. Food always came second to rent. He dreaded the day that it might be raised, and tried to keep aside a few extra pennies every week. He had promised his dying mother that he would look after his blind brother, and that meant keeping a roof over Sammy's head. Since Mutsy had learned so many tricks, more money had been coming in, and things had become easier.

Mutsy was a very clever dog. He was about two years old when he followed Alfie home one day from Smithfield Market, and from that first morning he could learn any trick that Alfie could think to teach him. Shaking hands, rolling over, carrying his tail, saying his prayers – all these things were easy as pie for Mutsy. But the best trick of all – and the one that earned Alfie's gang the most money – was Mutsy's 'singing dog' act.

Seen by the dim light coming in from the gas lamp on the street, Mutsy was no beauty. He was a big dog, bigger than most around, large and very hairy, with reddish brown fur, a fringe hanging over his eyes and enormous paws. Alfie guessed that he had a bit of a drover dog in him – the men that drove the cows and sheep from the country into the market at Smithfield sometimes had dogs like this. Since following Alfie that day six months after their parents had died, Mutsy had made his home with the boys in the cellar. His main duty was to take care of Sammy, but Alfie and he had a very special relationship, and it was Alfie who had taught him to sing and to do tricks.

'Wants the sausages,' said Jack, getting an affectionate lick from the dog.

'Nah, he's just pleased to see me, aren't you, old son? He knew that the peelers got hold of me. Anyways, he caught three rats this morning – huge ones, too. He won't be hungry for a while.' Alfie was glad to pause for a moment, enjoying a play fight with Mutsy. He would not admit it to the other gang members, but he had got quite a fright back there in the Bow Street Police Station, and an even greater fright just a moment before when he had seen the young Indian lurking across the street. While Jack's back was turned, he gave Mutsy a quick hug and kept his hand on the big dog's head as he followed Jack down the stairs into the cellar.

'What are you so scared about?' Sammy turned on his stool beside the fire, his blind eyes seeming to focus in on his brother.

'Scared? Me?' Alfie gave what he felt sounded like a convincing chuckle. He knew it was no good, though. Sammy had lost his eyesight when he had measles as a baby, but the loss of sight had doubled the sharpness of his hearing. Sammy could hear a feather fall from a bird in the street, Jack had once said and Alfie agreed with him.

'You are scared.' Sammy turned his blind eyes back to the fire. 'I could hear it the moment you spoke to Mutsy on the stairs.'

'Just playing with him.' Alfie busied himself with Mutsy, clenching his fists and dodging around and around, pretending to land blows on the dog. He wasn't going to admit to anyone, except perhaps to Mutsy, that he felt frightened. Stealing was all right – often, unless he stole, the gang would starve – but murder was a different matter.

'Got much for the singing?' he asked.

Sammy shrugged. 'Not much. You spoiled it with all the fuss over the bread van and the peelers blowing whistles.' His sensitive fingers felt among the coins of the tin plate in front of him and then stacked them neatly. 'Ten pennies, six half-pence and one bad thruppeny bit.'

'Enough for the beer – and some still left over for the rent money.'

Jack was already gathering up some of the coins. They knew that Alfie would say that. His parents had died of cholera one hot summer from drinking water that had been contaminated by the foul water leaking into the well from nearby cesspits. Alfie always made sure that he and his gang drank light small beer, no matter what else they had to go without. Beer was boiled for days and no badness could lurk in it. A young doctor had told Alfie that.

'Fry the sausages, Tom.' He tossed the packet to his younger cousin with a lordly air and then sat down by the fire. Mutsy's large head was heavy, but comforting, on his lap.

'Why do I always have to do the work?' complained Tom.

'Because I say you do.' Alfie didn't feel like arguing with his youngest cousin.

'What's up?' asked Sammy.

'You do keep on,' growled Alfie.

Mutsy looked from one face to the other. Behind his fringe, his soft brown eyes had a worried look. Alfie petted him absent-mindedly. Tom, muttering to himself, was busy with the spitting pan of sausages, Jack had gone for the beer. It was only himself and Sammy. Alfie decided to unburden himself; Sammy would get it out of him sooner or later.

'That inspector fellow,' he said abruptly. 'He let me off because he wants me to do something for him.' He stopped and gulped a little. Mutsy nuzzled him under the arm.

'It's a murder,' he continued. To himself his voice sounded off-hand, but he knew, from the alert way that Sammy turned his head, that he understood how nervous his brother was. 'He wants me to find the bloke that killed this rich man, Mr Montgomery – you know the people that Sarah works for in Bedford Square. The inspector thinks an Indian did it – one of those lascars from the East India Dock.' He stopped. He didn't know whether he should say any more, but both Mutsy and Sammy had their faces turned towards him so he continued. 'I saw an Indian just before I came in. He was across the road and looking at me. I'd say that he noticed the inspector letting me out of the police station.'

And now it was known. Alfie gave a hasty look towards Tom and then muttered in Sammy's ear, 'Not sure it's a good idea to be mixed up with murder.'

CHAPTER 6

ALFIE'S PLAN

Alfie counted the rent money and then paced restlessly up and down the cellar. He wished that Jack would come back with the beer. It was poor stuff, this small beer that they bought – no alcohol left in it really, but it had a sharp, clean flavour and it would go well with the sausages. He felt that he needed to clear his mouth of the taste of that police station and of the room where the dead bodies lay. He could still see the purple, swollen face of Mr Montgomery. Was it Betty who twisted that wire around his throat? Or did the Indian kill him? He gave Mutsy another hug and sat down beside his brother again.

'Likely the Indian meant you no harm,' said Sammy after a minute. 'Likely he wondered what you were doing in the police station. You'd be the same if you was him.'

'True enough.' A great weight was suddenly lifted off Alfie. He had not thought of the matter like that. 'There might be a reward,' he said. 'I got a shilling already.'

'Worth thinking about, ain't it?' Sammy's voice conveyed something to Mutsy, who gave a quick, sharp bark and then wagged his tail.

'Worth thinking about,' echoed Alfie. He looked at Sammy carefully. Although he was two years older, it was sometimes hard for Alfie to persuade Sammy to follow some of his plans. Sammy had to think it was a good idea. So when Alfie spoke, he was careful to keep his voice casual.

'I was thinking that if only Sarah could get me into the house, then I might find out something about them. Find out what's going on. She told me that they are looking for a knife boy for a week or so – seems their knife boy got badly burned when a pot of boiling fat tipped over on him. He landed himself in hospital. All I'd have to do is sit and clean knives all day, but I might pick up something.'

Sammy grinned. The smile lit up his face and almost sent a sparkle to his blind eyes.

'You needn't try to fool me,' he said. 'You were thinking that I might do it.'

Alfie chuckled. He couldn't help being proud of his brother. He was a sparky fellow.

'That's right,' he admitted. 'I thought you might. You'd get on well with Sarah's missus, too. Remember the time that she had you sing for her? We got a shilling out of that. And you'd get a good dinner in the middle of every day.' He stopped, but this was such an essential part of his plan that he forced himself to say the words that he would not normally have said. 'And you're a pretty spry fellow. You've got brains. You'll pick up all sorts of things. You'll hear what they sound like. You'll know if one of them sounds a bit uneasy.'

'And they won't be worried about what they say

in front of me,' mused Sammy. 'People don't when you're blind. They think it means that you're daft, as well.' He stretched out his hand. Mutsy came over to him and Sammy brushed the dog's fringe from the soft brown eyes.

Alfie watched. Sometimes he felt very bad about Sammy.

'Tom, them sausages are done,' he said decisively, looking away from Sammy and Mutsy and at the crisp brown sausages. 'Put the pan to one side. That's Jack coming now.'

And then Mutsy gave a quick, short bark and stood up, his furry tail very straight and one large paw lifted, every fibre in his body stiff and aggressive.

The door opened and in came Jack, carefully carrying the beer in a large jug.

But he wasn't alone.

Behind him was someone else.

Someone dark-skinned, hair covered in a white turban. He was tall and straight, but his hand trembled and the light flashed on something in that hand.

The Indian had come to meet them.

And he had a knife in his hand.

CHAPTER 7

THE DIAMOND RING

Alfie got to his feet quickly. His mouth was very dry. He could hear Jack gulp, and, as he approached the fire, his cousin's face showed white, with every freckle standing out sharply.

Of course, the Indian was probably a lascar, and those sailors always had a knife. But why had Jack allowed him in? He must have threatened him. Jack was as brave as a lion; in fact, sometimes Alfie thought that Jack was, by nature, much braver than he himself was, but Jack wasn't stupid. He wouldn't bring a stranger in unless he had been forced, and he wouldn't argue with a knife.

'Give us the beer, Jack.' Forcing himself to sound natural, Alfie kept a sharp eye on the Indian as he stretched out a hand for the beer. Carefully, though without looking at it, he set the jug on the box that they used as a table. Mutsy, he noticed, had gone over to Sammy and was standing beside him. He did not growl, but he was alert.

'Care for a sausage?' Alfie addressed the stranger in a casual way, but was disconcerted when a shake of the head refused the offer.

'What were you doing in the police station?' The Indian watched Alfie carefully. The fellow's English was good compared to other Indians that Alfie had known. Most of them worked on the boats that traded between London and India and they spoke only to their fellow lascars. This boy probably learned English when he and his father worked on Mr Montgomery's tea plantations.

'What's your name?' Alfie was pleased with the

sound of his voice. Only Sammy would guess that he was frightened.

The Indian paused. 'Mallesh.' He slid the knife up into his sleeve. Mutsy stretched out on the floor beside Alfie's cushion.

'Sit here next to my brother.' Alfie pulled out an old tattered cushion and placed it between Sammy and the fire. Now he could see Mallesh's face and Sammy could listen to his voice.

'You . . . you are blind.' Mallesh was looking at Sammy. His voice was hesitant, but Alfie could see a look of pity on his face.

'Yes,' agreed Sammy. He always preferred people to mention this straight away and not to be embarrassed. 'What do you want with Alfie?'

Only Sammy would have asked that question straight out, thought Alfie, and he could see how startled Mallesh was. For a moment the knife slid down, but then Mallesh looked into the milky-blue eyes, the white skin and the blond hair of the blind boy beside him, and pushed it back up his sleeve again. There was a long pause before he spoke.

'The police are looking for me,' he said in a hesitant

voice. 'They have asked your brother, Alfie, to find me.'

So this *was* the Indian boy the inspector had spoken of.

'How do you know?' Alfie could hear the note of panic in his own voice. Instinctively he put one hand on Mutsy's neck, kneading the powerful muscles under the loose, hairy skin.

'I listened outside the window. Outside the window of the police station. I heard everything.'

'Cor,' said Alfie with a nervous laugh, 'you must have a great pair of ears. You're as good as old Sammy here.'

'What were you doing listening at the police station?' Sammy stretched out until his hand met Mutsy's back and he, too, stroked the big dog. He turned his alert ear towards their visitor.

Mallesh hesitated. 'I wanted . . . to ask that man . . . that policeman . . . the one in charge. I wanted to ask him something . . .'

'Ask the inspector something? What?' queried Alfie.

There was a long silence. Mallesh seemed as if he were trying to make up his mind about something.

'Are you going to do what the inspector demanded?' he asked eventually. 'Help him find me?'

'Dunno.' Alfie leaned forward and tried staring at the visitor. This sort of stare usually worked well with local tough boys and it hid his nervousness.

'What's all this about?' asked Jack, always the peacemaker. He took down the pewter mugs from the shelf and put the frying pan on the floor by the fire. He skewered one of the sausages on the tip of a knife and handed it to Sammy, then took another one himself.

'Have one.' He pushed the pan a little towards Mallesh. 'And some bread.'

Mallesh shook his head again at the sausages, but readily cut a chunk from the loaf of bread, muttering '*Shukriya*'.

That must mean *thanks*, thought Alfie, listening with interest to the strange sound of this new language.

Mallesh thrust his knife into the crust and held it to the fire, moving it around so that it browned evenly. Jack's friendliness seemed to make him more relaxed.

'The inspector at Bow Street wants me to help him

solve the killing of that Mr Montgomery from Bedford Square,' said Alfie casually, biting into his own sausage. He ignored Mallesh and addressed his remark to Jack.

'You!' Tom took a sausage.

Alfie carefully shared the beer out between the four mugs, leaving some in the jug, which he offered to the visitor.

'He knows that your father was hanged by Mr Montgomery,' he said eventually, looking directly at Mallesh, who now seemed nervous and unsure. Quietly Alfie took the knife from Mallesh and placed another chunk of bread on it, and then put another sausage on Sammy's knife. He didn't go back to his own cushion, but sat on the floor, just beside his brother, with his knee touching Sammy's.

'He thinks that I murdered that man.' Mallesh's voice was calm and flat – just stating a fact.

Alfie took a deep breath. 'Did you murder Mr Montgomery?' he asked in an offhand tone.

Mallesh shook his head. '*Nahin*,' he said emphatically. 'I did not know that he was dead – not until I listened at the window. I just wanted the . . .' He

42

paused for a moment, hunting for the word, and then said, 'diamond'.

'From his ring? He had a diamond ring.'

'That's right – it was not his diamond.' Mallesh suddenly stopped. 'What's that?'

Footsteps were coming rapidly down the stairs, footsteps of someone running. Instantly, Mallesh was on his feet, his knife gleaming in his hand.

CHAPTER 8

A FOUL AND WICKED MAN

There was a moment's uneasy silence and then Sammy laughed. 'That's just Sarah,' he said. 'She needs to get her shoe mended. You can hear that one shoe is worn at the heel.'

Mutsy hadn't waited for Sammy's explanation. He was already by the door; there wasn't much light over there, but Alfie could hear the thumping of the tail on the old floorboards.

'Sarah's a friend,' he said reassuringly to Mallesh. He didn't think that he would mention that she was the scullery maid at Mr Montgomery's house.

Tom was already lifting the latch. Sarah came in, and stopped. Alfie could not see her face, but he guessed that she'd had a shock. It was not like Sarah to hang around near the door; normally she would come straight over to them. From where she stood, she would be able to see Mallesh very clearly by the light of the fire.

'Shut the door, Tom,' he said in what he hoped was a cheerful, reassuring tone. 'Come on in, Sarah. Have a sausage.'

Sarah didn't look very alarming, thought Alfie, though he kept an eye on Mallesh. She was small for twelve, wearing a cloak too big for her and a battered old bonnet that covered her brown hair. Her green eyes were huge in her thin face. The food was reasonable at the Montgomery house so Alfie guessed that she was just worked too hard. She had courage, though. Now, she ignored Mallesh and was shaking Mutsy by the paw and chatting cheerfully to him.

'How many rats today, old boy?' she asked. Mutsy

whined softly, then dashed over to the corner of the room and had a quick sniff before returning to her. He loved Sarah, but the word 'rats' was always enough to get him excited.

'Sit there.' Alfie nodded towards his cushion. 'Have a swig of my beer. Not too much – the sausages make me thirsty.'

'I brought a few handfuls of chestnuts,' said Sarah. 'They were left over and Cook said that I could have them.' Her eyes were still on Mallesh as she sat by the fire.

'You roast them, Tom,' said Alfie. 'You'd have some of these, Mallesh, wouldn't you?'

Mallesh nodded and once again muttered, '*Shukriya.*' His eyes were still on Sarah, but he had slipped his knife on to his belt.

'I saw you before,' he said hesitantly. 'At the Montgomery house, was that it? In the yard at the back . . .'

'That's right.' Sarah looked back at him directly.

'Mallesh is just going to tell us the story of his father, and how Mr Montgomery had him hanged,' said Alfie and was pleased when Sarah said nothing.

'Wrongly hanged, bad justice!' said Mallesh. He banged his fist on the floor, making Tom's head swivel. A chestnut escaped the spoon and hopped on to the ground. Mutsy sniffed it carefully, but the others did not move.

'Murdered,' continued Mallesh.

'Tell us about it,' commanded Alfie.

'My father found a diamond. He found it when he dug a well next to our house. He had to break up the stone to get down to clean water and he saw something bright. He went to Montgomery-Sahib with it and the Sahib pretended that he is going to get the value. Got a man to look and say the value . . .'

No one said anything. Mallesh's voice was so full of rage that the words came out in broken sentences, mixed with words from his own language.

'Rubbish and lies . . . *Zyaada kuch nahi* . . . He told my father the diamond expert said it's no good . . . worthless . . . just a piece of glass. And then the officers came . . . the law people . . . my father was dragged off to prison.'

One by one the chestnuts had hopped. Tom put them carefully into an iron pot, but he didn't move or offer them around. Mutsy put his head on Mallesh's foot.

'What was your father accused of?' asked Alfie. Mallesh's story fitted so far with what the inspector had told him.

'He was accused of stealing a bag of coins – no words said about the diamond. I begged my mother and my uncle to ask about the diamond, but they would not. They were too scared. And my father was hanged.'

'What happened to you?' asked Sarah. She sounded sorry for him, and Mallesh gave her a quick, grateful look.

'I ran away that very day. I went to Calcutta and got a job on a ship. I've been on ships ever since . . . for the last year.'

'And how did you find where Mr Montgomery lived?' asked Alfie.

'My father told me that Montgomery-Sahib had a big house in a city called London, in a place called Bedford Square. He explained it all to me in Hindu language. I pictured it a big, square house when he told me what it meant.' Mallesh smiled a little to himself.

Perhaps he found London very strange, thought Alfie. He would have liked to ask more questions but said nothing as Mallesh continued.

'Last week when we came to East India Docks, a lascar shouts, "Two crates of tea for Montgomery, number one, Bedford Square." I followed the cart and I found Montgomery-Sahib.'

'Why did you go there, go to the house?' Would he get a truthful answer to that question, wondered Alfie.

The answer came quickly. 'I just wanted to see him.'

'And did you see him?' Alfie kept his voice low and soothing. He didn't want that knife to come out again, though perhaps he and Jack might be able to manage the fellow. Still, Sammy might get hurt if there was a fight.

Mallesh nodded. '*Haan*, I —'

The word was hardly out of his mouth before Sarah said firmly, 'You must have seen him. I saw you yesterday hanging around near the mews and around the gatekeeper's lodge.'

'You got a look at the ring, then – some time when

Mr Montgomery was going out?' Alfie slipped the question in quickly, before the Indian boy could deny it.

Mallesh said nothing for a moment, but then he nodded. 'Yes, I did. I saw him hand a piece of money to the man at the gate. He took off his glove to get out a coin and I saw the ring. I'm sure that it is the stone that my father found.'

'You must have felt like murdering him!'

There was silence, and Alfie glared at Tom. That was the trouble with Tom, he thought. A good lad, fun to be with, great shot, could climb anything, but he always did speak before he thought. Alfie stayed very quiet himself and so did everyone else. Tom glanced from one to the other and then gave the pot of chestnuts a quick toss.

'I am not the murderer,' said Mallesh firmly. 'I tell you. I didn't even know he was dead. I heard it first when the policeman talked to you.'

'But what were you doing hanging around the police station?' asked Alfie. The more he thought about that, the more it puzzled him.

'It was my friend's idea,' explained Mallesh. 'He

keeps a lodging house at the East India Docks, a lodging house for lascars. He told me that in England if you want justice you go to a police station. He told me that you know a police station by the blue light outside the door.'

'So why didn't you go in?' asked Alfie.

'I wanted to see what kind of man he is. So I listened at the window. '

'So that was the way of it,' said Jack. His broad, friendly face shone with a liking of Mallesh. Alfie wondered if he could trust Jack's judgement. His quiet cousin, though friendly, wasn't easily taken in.

'That's right,' said Mallesh. 'I listened to him. I heard him say Mr Montgomery was found dead this morning. I heard him ask you to find me, and I think, you are a poor boy, like me; I can talk to you.'

'But you weren't the one that croaked Mr Montgomery, were you?' Alfie made a quick gesture with his hand to mime a strangling.

Mallesh shook his head.

'Swear,' ordered Alfie. 'Say I swear by all that is holy. Say you swear by —'

'By Almighty God,' said Sammy. He was an

authority on church matters. He went to church every Sunday to learn the hymns and the Christmas carols.

'*Sogand xwardan.*' Mallesh said the words solemnly, placing his two hands together and bowing.

Alfie's knee touched his brother's and Sammy nodded his fair head. His hand found Alfie's, and gave it a quick squeeze. Alfie knew what he meant. Sammy had heard truth in Mallesh's voice.

But if Mallesh was innocent, who *was* the murderer?

Alfie looked at Sarah and found she was looking at him, her green eyes sharp and intelligent. She didn't look as if she disbelieved Mallesh, more as if she was considering other matters.

'Anyone in the house that could have murdered him?' Alfie asked her casually.

Sarah grinned, her small teeth flashing in the firelight. She held up one hand.

'Three,' she said, counting on her fingers. 'I make it three.'

'Three!' echoed Tom, quickly eating the last sausage and then coming to sit by Jack. 'Who are they?'

'No one wanted him home,' said Sarah. 'Nora, the parlour maid, told me that. It was all right when he came for a short holiday, but then he decided to stay permanently and he cramped the style of the missus, no end. She was used to suiting herself, and now he was giving the orders and telling her what to do. Then there was the son, Mr Denis. Nora says that he is a gambler. He goes to this betting club in Leicester Square, and there's been big quarrels with the father about that – his mother adores him and he got money easily out of her.'

'And who's the third?' asked Jack.

Sarah took a quick look at the slit of window that showed the feet of the passers-by, and when she spoke her voice was so low that Alfie had to lean forward to hear her.

'It's the butler,' she said, her face full of fear. 'I wouldn't be surprised if he committed a murder. He's a violent man. And he would have a reason. Nora says he's been selling bits of the family's silver for years – spoons, the odd dish, that sort of thing. Mr Montgomery had a huge row with him and said he was going to report him to the police.' Her voice shook and then she added, 'But for God's sake, don't ever tell anyone that I told you. He's a foul and wicked man and he'd kill me as easy as you break the neck of a chicken.'

CHAPTER 9

HOMELESS?

There was a long silence after Sarah's words. Finally Jack spoke.

'If you can find out something, the inspector will give you a few bob, is that right, Alfie?'

Alfie nodded and took charge. 'That means that we must all put our brains together and see if we can solve this murder,' he said. 'Mallesh says that he didn't do it and we believe him, so who did do it?

What about the missus, Sarah?'

'What?! A woman go along Monmouth Street and strangle her husband? Very likely!' said Tom scornfully.

Alfie gave him a long, cold stare. 'Who said she would do it herself, numbskull? She'd hire someone to do it, of course. There are fifty men at St Giles who would murder for the price of a pint of beer.'

'He's right, though, Alfie.' Sarah was looking thoughtful. 'I can't see the missus going down to St Giles and finding someone to do a murder for her.'

'Would she have a man friend?' asked Jack.

Sarah shook her head. 'I wouldn't know,' she said. 'I never go upstairs. I wouldn't know unless Nora, the parlour maid, told me. Sometimes she tells me things, like about the butler, but she probably wouldn't tell me things about the lady of the house. It's possible, though. A couple of times in the stables I saw a beautiful black horse and the coachman told me that it belonged to a Mr Peters who was paying Mrs Montgomery a visit. I haven't seen it since Mr Montgomery came home.'

'Doesn't mean she didn't meet him somewhere

else, though,' said Alfie thoughtfully.

'What about the son?' asked Jack. 'What do you know about him, Sarah?'

'Mr Denis is a big, tall man with a big loud voice. I heard him shouting at his father once when I was scrubbing the front doorstep.'

'What was he saying?' Alfie was immediately interested in this. Denis Montgomery sounded a more likely suspect than Mrs Montgomery.

'He was saying something about being ruined,' said Sarah.

'Ruined?' Mallesh was puzzled.

'I think he meant that he had no money to pay his debts, to pay back money that he borrowed,' explained Sarah. 'If what the parlour maid says is true, he goes out gambling – do you understand that, Mallesh? It means that he bets on things like horse races, or on playing cards or throwing dice, and if he doesn't guess right he loses his money.'

'Funny a rich man being too mean to give money to his son,' said Tom. 'I wouldn't fancy having a father like him.'

'Let's try to guess who did do it,' said Alfie.

'Sammy, you've been very quiet. Who do you think?'

'I'm not going to guess,' said Sammy. 'I'd like to wait until I hear them speak, and then I'll know, perhaps.'

'I think it was the butler – he was in big trouble,' said Sarah.

'I'll say Mrs Montgomery got a friend to do it,' said Jack.

'I'll go for Denis,' said Alfie. 'He's definitely the most likely.'

'But why would he offer a reward then?' Tom piped up.

Alfie narrowed his eyes at Tom. 'That's just to put people off the scent.'

'Perhaps Mr Montgomery stole something from someone, or . . .' Mallesh moved his hands in circles as he looked for a word.

'Or cheated someone,' suggested Sarah.

'*Haan,*' said Mallesh nodding his head. 'That's the word.'

'Someone that we don't know about yet,' mused Alfie. 'I wonder . . .'

'I'll go for Sarah, the scullery maid,' said Tom with a grin. 'She got fed up with him putting dirty footprints on her clean step so she murdered him.'

'Stop being stupid,' said Alfie. 'You just keep saying stupid things and —'

A thunderous knock interrupted him.

They all looked at each other. Mallesh jumped up and then stood hesitating, the knife gleaming in his hand.

'Hide,' whispered Sarah. She grasped him by the arm and pushed him into a dark corner away from the fire. 'Lie down and I'll put some cushions over you,' she hissed.

Alfie nodded, and when there was no sign of Mallesh to be seen, he strolled over to the door. 'Who's there?' he called as a tremendous thump showed that their visitor had kicked the door.

'It's me, your landlord. Open up, or I'll kick this door down and you'll pay for the mending of it.'

Alfie hastened to obey the order. Mr Parker would do what he threatened.

'I've already paid your rent-collector on Saturday,' he said as he unlocked the door. To his annoyance he heard his voice tremble.

'No, you haven't. Rents have gone up. You owe

me an extra bob. Think yourself lucky that it isn't a crown. It's not many people who would let out a lovely comfortable cellar like this to a pack of kids.'

And charge them double the rent, thought Alfie. He said nothing, though. They all had to keep a roof over their heads, and he would just have to pay the extra. He went over to the shelf, took down the rent jar and emptied it out into his hand.

'One, two, three, four, five, six, seven, eight, nine, ten, eleven, twelve pennies,' he said aloud. Half of next week's rent. Now that was gone, and next week he would have to find three shillings or thirty-six pennies for this old scoundrel. And perhaps the week after the rent would double again . . .

'Here you are, Mr Parker. This leaves us without food tomorrow,' he said, trying to keep his voice steady. He felt like kicking or punching or even screaming. But he just stood quietly until the door had been slammed shut, and then went back to sit beside Sammy. He dared not trust his voice for the moment, so he just sat there, staring into the fire and allowing Sammy to rest his arm on his shoulder. No one else spoke; they were all waiting for him.

Eventually he gave Sammy a little push, sat up straight and looked around, doing his best to make his voice cheerful and confident.

'Well, that's it, then. We must solve that murder and get the rent money from the inspector. Otherwise we'll all be out in the street. And winter is coming on!'

CHAPTER 10

A SPY IN
THE HOUSE

It almost seemed as though dawn had not yet come the following morning when Sammy and Alfie left Bow Street and walked up Monmouth Street towards Bloomsbury. The street was dark and the air was filled with fog so thick, it almost seemed like a solid wall in front of them. Sammy's hair, carefully washed and brushed by Alfie, was now standing up from his head in tight curls. He walked along whistling quietly to himself, apparently quite relaxed and happy, but Alfie was worried. Perhaps he should never have suggested putting his blind brother into that house. Sarah's words and her frightened face kept coming into his mind.

'Do you want me to do it instead, Sam?' he said, stopping abruptly outside a shop in Monmouth Street, and then moving on hurriedly when he realised from the police posters in the window that he had stopped on the very spot where Mr Montgomery had been garrotted.

'Nah,' said Sammy placidly. 'I'll enjoy it. Bit of a change for me. Won't be many people around today. No point in me singing in this fog.'

Funny how Sammy always knew what the weather was like and what sort of a day it was going to be, thought Alfie, trying to move his thoughts away from the butler and from what Sarah had said: *he's a foul and wicked man.*

Bedford Square had three sides of tall brick-built houses, all with huge chimneys and impressive front doors behind the tall white pillars framing the porches. Leafless creepers grew up many of them, and in the centre of the square was a garden filled with dead leaves and bare shrubs.

The fourth side of the square had high, black railings and a double gate. Both gate and railings had spikes on them and there was a small lodge for a porter beside the gate. Alfie gazed at the splendour for a moment and then tucked his arm inside Sammy's.

'Back entrance for us, old son,' he said cheerfully. 'Only posh gents and ladies come into the square through the front gate.'

'Did you see number one?' Sammy sounded unconcerned.

'Yes, it's the closest to us. Ah, there are the mews for the horses and the carriages at the back of the houses.' Alfie chatted on, as he always did, doing his best to be Sammy's eyes in the dark world that his brother inhabited. 'Hang on,' there's a small door here. Let's go in, yes, we're just behind the house now. We'll just go down the steps here into the basement. That's what Sarah said.'

'Here she is,' Sammy exclaimed, and then Sarah appeared looking worried and even paler than usual.

'Come on in,' she whispered. 'The housekeeper

remembers Mrs Montgomery listening to Sammy singing on the street and getting her coachman to bring him here. She says that Mrs Montgomery will have to see him for herself and then decide.'

Alfie pulled off his own cap and Sammy's, and then followed her into the kitchen, which seemed full of women wearing various types of aprons.

'This is the boy, Mrs Higgins.' Sarah gave a quick bob of a curtsy.

'She's very charitable, the missus, taking on a blind boy.' The housekeeper slightly lowered her voice – just as if I were deaf as well as blind, thought Sammy – and then raised it again. 'Better go and tell her that he's here, Nora. She said she wanted to see him when he arrived. Said it would take her mind off her sorrow.'

There was a slightly sarcastic note in the voice. Sammy wondered whether Alfie had noted it.

'She's got that inspector from Bow Street with her.' So that was Nora, the parlour maid – Sammy knew he would recognise her voice again, pretending to be posh, but London cockney underneath.

'He's to go into the breakfast parlour; the Missus said to take him straight in. She'll be finished with the inspector by then, more than likely.'

Or else she wants to show the inspector what a nice, kind lady she is, thought Sammy. At the very same moment he felt Alfie nudge him and knew that it had occurred to his brother, too – that Mrs Montgomery would probably like the inspector to think that a woman who would take on a blind boy as a member of her staff would be incapable of murdering her husband.

'I'll come with you.' There was a tremor in Alfie's confident, slightly cheeky voice that only Sammy would hear. He wouldn't like these posh places, Sammy knew. Alfie liked to be the top dog. He wouldn't want anyone looking down on him.

'No, you won't. Off with you.' The parlour maid sounded definite. Sammy pressed Alfie's hand lightly. Trust me, his fingers said.

As the door banged shut behind his brother, Sammy remembered what Alfie had said to him. *Listen to Mrs Montgomery. Listen to the butler, too. But I still reckon that son of theirs, Denis, is the most likely. It suited him to murder his father – after all, he was in debt and his father was probably not too keen on him hanging around with no job and up to his eyes in debt. He's more likely to be the one that croaked the old man, not Mallesh, whatever the police think.*

'You come with him too, Sarah. The boy knows you.' Nora said no more until they had climbed the stairs leading up from the kitchen and were walking across a tiled floor, the two girls' heels clicking and Sammy's bare feet feeling the cool, well-polished surface.

'Tidy that scarf of his, Sarah, and flatten down these curls.'

Sammy stood very still while Sarah busied herself. He could hear Mrs Montgomery's voice from inside the breakfast parlour. Even to him it was faint – no one but Sammy could have heard anything – but after a while he made out the words.

' . . . been four years as a butler to me,' she was saying. 'I would never have suspected him, but Mr Montgomery was suspicious. There seemed to be a lot of silver missing. He gave the butler one week to find it, and said that if it had not turned up in that time, the police would be called.'

Unfortunately at that moment Nora knocked sharply on the door and there was a silence, followed by a high, sweet voice calling them to come in.

'So here is little Sammy!' Mrs Montgomery said *Sammy* as if he were her favourite lap dog. Sammy hoped she wouldn't try to kiss him. Letting go of Nora's hand, he moved into the room. Mrs Montgomery sounded just as she had done the last time he came. Her high voice was as clear as ever. She hadn't been doing much crying, he thought. Sammy knew well how crying could affect the voice. The room smelled of furniture polish, there was a soft carpet and curtains at the windows, he guessed – the clip-clop of horses' hooves outside was muted. Lots of cushions and soft chairs, too, probably; the air felt like that – dead, somehow. Nice and warm, though. The chimney had been swept and the coal smelled clean.

'Oh, Inspector, this poor little boy is blind and starving, so I have decided to offer him a job as a knife boy. He will get a good meal every day and three shillings at the end of the week. And, do you know, Inspector, he sings like an angel!'

'Shall I sing a song for you, ma'am?'

Mrs Montgomery was getting nearer to him; if he didn't stop her, she would undoubtedly kiss him –

especially as Alfie had cleaned him up and dressed him in fairly decent clothes from the second-hand shop. Without waiting for an answer, Sammy broke into the first verse of a hymn that he had learned at St Martin's church: '*Now the day is over . . .*'

'Beautiful,' said Mrs Montgomery when he had finished.

'Beautiful.' That must be the inspector, a tough man, by the sound of his voice. He was probably afraid that Sammy would sing again, and delay him longer from his enquiries; his voice sounded hurried when he said quickly, 'And now, perhaps I could have a word with your son, Mr Denis Montgomery? I also understand there is another gentleman staying here, a Mr Scott, your late husband's partner in his Indian tea plantation.'

'That's right, Inspector. My husband decided to retire – he was enjoying life in London – so Mr Scott came over to wind up their business affairs. He planned to stay here for a few weeks and then return to India.'

'And could I see him, and your son?'

Mrs Montgomery gave a little laugh. She sounded nervous. Sammy listened carefully as she continued,

'I'm afraid that neither gentleman has come down for breakfast yet, Inspector. You'll have to come back in an hour or so if you want to meet them.'

'Or better still, tell them to report to Bow Street Police Station at eleven o'clock this morning, ma'am. And now I'll bid you good day.' He hesitated for a moment and then slipped a coin into Sammy's hand – a four-penny groat by the feel of it, thought Sammy as he pocketed it, wondering whether the Inspector knew that he was Alfie's brother. He could still taste the sausages of the previous night and decided that it would be good to work for this inspector.

'Well, goodbye, Inspector.' Mrs Montgomery sounded glad to be rid of him. Perhaps she didn't really want her husband's murderer caught. Sammy could hear a note of relief in her voice once the door had closed behind the inspector and she sounded more cheerful as she said, 'Nora, take the boy into the butler's pantry. He can work in there. Find him an apron to put over his clothes. Go along, Sammy, dear. I'm sure that you will work hard and do your best. Remember to keep very quiet when the two gentlemen come in for breakfast. Nora, tell the chambermaid to bring up the gentlemen's hot water for shaving and give them Inspector Denham's message.'

And then they were outside the room and Sammy felt his way cautiously down the stairs again. Nora smelled strongly of soap, and it was easy to follow her back into the kitchen.

'I have to find Becky and give her the message. Sarah, you look after the boy and keep him out of trouble.' Nora's heels clicked away down the hall.

CHAPTER 11

A MYSTERIOUS CONVERSATION

'So all you have to do, Sammy, is take each knife, one by one, out of the water.' Sammy was sitting in the butler's pantry, with Sarah by his side. 'Then stick it into this bowl of emery powder here, just by your right hand. Rub the knife with the damp cloth until all the powder is off and then polish it with this bit of baize. Then place it into this knife box here with the handle pointing to yourself.' Sarah was quick and sensible in her instructions. Sammy could feel the gritty emery powder, the cold wetness of the damp cloth and the smooth softness of the baize cloth, as she moved his hand from one thing to another. The knife box was also lined with baize, he thought, feeling its divisions carefully.

'I'll come in and out as often as I can. I can come up by the back stairs, behind where you are sitting – they're for the servants – and I'll make sure you're doing it right. You'll soon get the hang of it. Don't worry about the butler – he will be out this morning delivering mourning cards for the funeral. The two gentlemen still have to come for their breakfast, Nora says. You be as quiet as you can, but don't worry too much about them hearing you because the door is double-lined with baize.' And then she was gone and Sammy settled to work, wiping the knives with the emery powder, backwards and forwards, testing carefully with his forefinger, rubbing each knife to a high gloss.

After a while, he heard one man come into the breakfast parlour next door, settle into a chair and noisily clear his throat. Then he heard the sound of liquid being poured into a cup, and a slight clang of metal. That would be a lid being replaced on a silver dish. Sarah had made the boys' mouths water when she told them of these dishes of eggs, sausages, bacon and kippers, all set out on top of their individual little heaters. This man was helping himself to a big breakfast – Sammy counted five little clangs. Next came the sound of the newspaper being unfolded and then nothing but the rustle of pages being turned and the noise of the man munching toast.

And then the door opened again. Someone came in; Sammy could swear to that. A man, judging by the weight of the footsteps.

But oddly there was no greeting spoken.

Nothing. Almost as if they were both there, just staring at each other.

And then a throat cleared. Not the first man. This man cleared his throat differently – lightly and almost apologetically, almost 'ahem, ahem.'

And then a voice . . .

Was this the first or the second man? Sammy thought it was the second. The voice, like the throat clearing, was slightly hesitant, slightly unsure.

'You found Coutts Bank open yesterday, sir?'

There was something strange about the query – as if something unspoken were lurking beneath. However, the speaker was obviously not Mr Denis, or Mr Scott. The accent was wrong for a toff. Sammy was good on accents. He had spent so much time singing outside the Covent Garden Theatre that he knew how toffs talked. This must be the butler, thought Sammy.

'Yes.' The one-word reply was harsh and abrupt, the voice of someone with power. This might be the son of the house, Mr Denis Montgomery, a man brought up surrounded by servants. Or was it Mr Scott from India?

And then no more was said.

Sammy strained his ears. Sarah was right about the double-lined baize door. Even for someone with his marvellous hearing, it was difficult to catch every word.

There were no more words, but there was a sound. It was not the clink of lids; it was the sound of money being counted out on to the table.

Sammy got up carefully and silently and moved

towards the door, hands outstretched to make sure that he did not touch any obstacle. It was agonising, expecting at any moment to stumble over a chair or to overbalance a small table, but he reached the door successfully, his sensitive fingers feeling the softness of its baize lining. He stayed very still, trying to control his breathing.

Listening . . .

And then another softer sound.

For a moment Sammy could not identify it, but then he realised that it was the gentle swish of coins being swept across a linen cloth and next – he was sure that he was right in this – being dropped into a waistcoat pocket.

After that, footsteps crossed the room again. The door opened and was shut quietly.

Sammy did not move. Why did the first man give money in this silent way to the second man? And what was the reason for the question about Coutts Bank? Unless, of course, that the second man had already asked for the money – perhaps he was a blackmailer. Perhaps he asked for more than the other carried around with him, and that was the reason for the question about the bank . . .

Sammy's agile mind played with the problem while the first man continued to chomp on his toast, swill his drink and rustle his newspaper and it seemed a long time before anything else happened. Sammy stayed where he was, though. His fingers found the keyhole to the baize door and when he heard the door of the breakfast parlour open again, he bent his head down so that he could listen better.

This time the footsteps had a different tread. A third man! The shoes trod the carpeted floor confidently, greetings were exchanged, lids banged, something poured out into a cup – coffee, thought Sammy, immediately identifying the odour. There was a coffee house in Bow Street; he had always thought the smell of that drink, spilling out on to the pavement, was wonderful.

Which man was which? he wondered. One man had a high voice and laughed a lot and the other had a deep voice and said very little. The trouble was that each man addressed the other as 'sir'. So which was Mr Denis Montgomery and which was Mr Scott, the partner in the dead man's enterprise in India? And which was the man who had spoken with the butler?

Sammy listened carefully, but not much was said. The conversation all seemed to be about the newspaper, plays at the Covent Garden Theatre, and Queen Victoria paying a visit somewhere. Nothing of interest.

He wasn't wasting his time, though – he would have something to tell Alfie. Both men were afraid. Dogs could smell fear, they said, but Sammy knew that he was almost as good as a dog – he could always hear tension in a voice, no matter how low the tone.

What had they both to be afraid of?

CHAPTER 12

THE SMELL OF FEAR

The morning passed slowly in the butler's pantry. Sammy was uneasy. There had been some sort of blackmail attempt earlier; he was sure of that. He didn't like to think what might happen if one or both of those men discovered that there had been a witness to their meeting,

At twelve o'clock, Sarah came to fetch him down to the kitchen for his midday meal. This was a nice mutton hash pie and the cook was good to him, telling Sarah to put plenty of food on his plate and giving him a slice of cake and drink of milk to finish up with. Sammy felt as if he wouldn't need to eat for a week.

But when Sammy returned to work in the butler's pantry he still felt troubled – and bored. He was glad when Sarah came in to whisper to him that he was wanted in the drawing room to help Mrs Montgomery choose a hymn to be sung at her husband's funeral.

'Can you check the knives first, Sarah?' Sammy got thankfully to his feet and stretched. He hoped he wouldn't have to go on too long with this knife cleaning. It was deadly dull compared to wandering around the streets, his hand on the loop of rope around Mutsy's collar, stopping to sing from time to time, collecting money for the gang, or chatting to some of the street-sellers. Or else Alfie or one of the others would join up with him and get Mutsy to do some tricks. Sammy always liked to hear the people laughing.

'They're fine, all of them. You've done a good job. Come on, now,' whispered Sarah. Her small rough hand led him down the back stairs – no carpet, there – too good for servants, Sammy supposed. 'Here he is, Nora.'

'You go off and finish those pans, Sarah, or Cook will be furious. I'll take the boy upstairs.' This was Nora. She sounded bossy, thought Sammy, feeling sorry for Sarah.

'Don't speak until you are spoken to in the drawing room.' Nora was keeping pace beside him on the stairs up to the first floor. She sounded unfriendly, but she did take the edge of his sleeve when he reached the top step and guided him to the door, knocking gently on it.

'Come in. Ah, Sammy. Well, how has he worked, Nora?' Mrs Montgomery was a distance from him, probably sitting at the piano.

'Very well, I believe, madam.'

'Good. Sammy has been working away in the butler's pantry cleaning the knives all day.' Mrs Montgomery obviously gave this piece of information to someone in the room, but there was only a grunt in reply.

'And now, Sammy, I want you to help me to select a hymn for my dear, dear husband's funeral service . . .'

Here there was an audible sniff and a slight rustle

as if the lady had taken out her pocket-handkerchief. It all rang false to Sammy's ear. He was fairly certain now that Mrs Montgomery had not cared too much for her husband. There was something forced and unnatural about the few sobs she produced.

'I want to hear how the hymns sound in a boy's voice. Bloomsbury church has a wonderful boys' choir, though I'm not sure whether you haven't a better voice than the chief chorister.'

'Thank you, ma'am,' said Sammy politely. He was interested to hear how natural and brisk her voice sounded once she had ceased sobbing into her handkerchief.

'Denis, dear, are you paying attention? Mr Scott, I would value your opinion, also.'

So the two of them were in the room. Neither man replied and that was annoying. Presumably they had just nodded. He wished that he could have had another chance to hear their voices, to work out which one of them had had that odd conversation with the butler. Sammy had sensed one man quite near to where he stood, but the other must have been at the end of the room, because footsteps approached. And there was the sound of a heavy body sinking into an armchair. A waft of some slightly odd smell too.

'I can't make up mind between "Abide with Me" and "Rock of Ages",' said Mrs Montgomery. 'Let's try "Abide with Me". I'll teach you the first verse and then we'll try it out.'

'I know it, ma'am,' said Sammy respectfully. That particular song had been a great favourite of his grandfather, and it was always popular when sung outside the theatre when the late night crowd was milling around waiting for a cab.

'Wonderful!' said Mrs Montgomery when he had finished. 'Goodness, what a marvellous voice! I think this will be my choice. We'll just try that again in a higher key. Nora, open the door so that everyone in the house can hear.'

And then, less than one minute after the high C broke from Sammy's lips, there was a scrabble and a skidding noise from the hallway, a thumping of paws on the stairs, a sudden pungent smell of dog in the scented room and an ear-splitting howl. Mutsy had joined in the hymn.

Mrs Montgomery screamed.

One man shouted and the other laughed . . . And then Sarah was in the room, stammering out apologies again and again. She had just opened the back door, she said, and the dog had got in, dashed up the passageway, passing through the swinging doors with ease and then up the stairs. Sammy had stopped singing instantly. Sarah sounded terrified. He had to do something.

'Mutsy,' he said sternly. 'You should be ashamed of yourself!'

Before the last word was out of his mouth, Mutsy hit the carpet with a thud. He would be lying on his back with his two front paws covering his eyes, Sammy knew. Alfie had taught him this trick; the big dog would peep out from time to time and then cover his eyes again.

It never failed on the street and it didn't fail now. There was a loud braying noise from one man, a deep laugh from the other, and a little trilling laugh, instantly suppressed, from Mrs Montgomery – even Nora gave a discreet little chuckle. Only Sarah didn't laugh, and Sammy heard her catch her breath as if she were still panic-stricken.

'I'm sorry, Madam,' she said again.

'It's not Sarah's fault,' said Sammy. 'Mutsy is used to looking after me; he heard me singing, I suppose, and he thought he should come to me. He sings with me in the street. He never leaves me. He was probably waiting outside the back door for me.' Sammy knew that Tom was supposed to meet him, so Mutsy must have escaped from him.

'So that's what it was.' Mrs Montgomery sounded amused, but then rapidly returned to the deeper, tragic tone of someone whose husband has just been murdered. 'Well, Sammy, perhaps it would be best if you took the dog out. Go on, girl – take them downstairs. You've done enough for today, Sammy. You can go home now.'

And then he, Mutsy and Sarah were going down the stairs slowly, while Nora ran down lightly ahead of them.

'You can wait for Tom in the back kitchen,' whispered Sarah in his ear as Nora's footsteps disappeared down a long corridor.

'Sarah, bring the boy in for something to eat. Cook says she's just made some cakes – and she's got a bone for the dog,' Nora called back. She sounded friendlier now. Her voice had a little chuckle in it. She must have told the story in the kitchen to the amusement of everyone. For a moment, Sammy felt sorry for the dead man. It didn't seem as if anyone in the house was particularly upset about his death. Obediently he followed Sarah, who had pushed open a door with a slight squeak.

Sammy's hand had just felt the baize lining – they must be going to the servants' part of the house – when he heard a man's voice – a harsh, menacing posh voice – from above on the landing. 'Was that boy in the butler's pantry all the morning?'

Was this the man who talked with the butler? Sammy thought so. He could almost sense waves of hatred – or was it fear – coming down the stairs. His scalp prickled and, in spite of the heat of the stove in the hallway, he felt a cold shiver go down his back.

CHAPTER 13

FOOTSTEPS IN THE FOG

It was a relief to be out of that house, although he had enjoyed the cake and Mutsy, he knew, had enjoyed the bone. Sammy was tired of that closed-in, perfumed smell and he was worried about the man with the harsh voice – was he the murderer? The more that Sammy thought about it, the less he liked the thought of going back to the house the following morning.

He patted Mutsy's large head, took a deep breath of air and then coughed. There was a terribly thick fog out this afternoon, he reckoned. He jumped slightly as he heard an angry shout and the squeal of a horse that had been pulled up suddenly. The fog must be so bad that people crossing the road couldn't even see the cabs. He grinned to himself – Tom must have got lost. This was one time when he and Mutsy were better off than the people who could see. Mutsy just needed his nose and he, Sammy, had his two ears that were twice as good as anyone else's.

Mutsy was going home by a short cut, Sammy guessed. Now they seemed to be in one of those small courts around St Giles church. Sammy could sense the tall buildings – rookeries, they were known as – all around him. Thousands of people lived crowded together in those rookeries. Despite the fog, the air was full of the usual screams and shouts and curses and bangs. Under it all, though, he could hear something else. The fog muted the sound; nevertheless it was definitely the clip-clop of a horse. And the strange thing was that the horse was not trotting, but was walking slowly – walking as if the owner was following something, rather than making his way home as quickly as possible through the fog. And it was walking just behind him.

Sammy shrank in towards the wall, Mutsy's solid body between him and the horse that was following so closely.

There was a growl from Mutsy. Sammy acted instinctively and let go of the rope handle around Mutsy's neck. If something attacked, he didn't want to prevent Mutsy defending himself.

But there was no barking or snarling, just a sharp crack, a whimper and the sound of something heavy slumping to the ground.

And then a hand grabbed Sammy by the hair and unmercifully hauled him up. Sammy screamed. The pain from his scalp was unbearable, but it was terror that made him shriek. It was no good, though; he knew that as soon as the sound left his throat. No one in St Giles would ever notice a child screaming. Desperately he drummed with his heels. He was being pulled up on to the horse's back. He could smell the leather saddle, the well-groomed horse smell and the smell of a man – a man who had washed

and shaved with some sort of strange, exotic soap –
but something else, as well. A strong, clean sort of
smell . . .

Then Sammy's heart almost stopped. Around his
throat was something sharp that dug into the skin and
that choked the sound.

Frantically he scrabbled with his nails to remove
the razor-thin wire from his throat.

He could feel his fingers bleed as the noose tightened. The warm blood ran down his neck. He leaned
over to one side, trying to throw himself from the
horse's back. He would risk being trampled if he
managed it, but he didn't care. He knew that he was
in deadly danger. And what about Mutsy? Poor
Mutsy. As clearly as if he had have seen the whole
thing, Sammy knew that Mutsy, his protector, had
been hit on the head by a cudgel. Perhaps he was
dead. Sammy felt the tears run down his face as he
struggled with the wire.

And then he got a sharp blow to the side of his face.
The pain made him feel sick and giddy. His hands
loosened. The man on the horse pulled them away.
Now there was nothing to stop him being garrotted –

just like Mr Montgomery had been garrotted.

Perhaps in the same place, too! They were out of St Giles, now, Sammy reckoned, and were probably at Seven Dials. The paved road there had a hollow sound. People said that was because a great treasure was buried there before the tall pillar with its seven sundials had been built on this spot. Seven roads branched off from this central space, but the man on the horse went steadily ahead, so they must be going down Monmouth Street.

Sammy felt a cold trickle of sweat run down his back. If Mutsy did not come quickly there would be no hope for him. His body would be dropped in a dark doorway, just like the body of Mr Montgomery.

Then he heard the sharp shrill sound of a policeman's whistle. Shouts of 'Stop thief!' echoed from the walls of the tall houses on either side. There was a banging of doors and a rush of feet coming up from the cellars where the shoemakers of Monmouth Street worked. The quiet street was instantly alive with people.

Sammy's heart thudded with excitement. Surely one of the policemen, or even one of the crowd, rushing to the scene, would spot him. Perhaps in another moment he would be on his feet . . .

Suddenly a rug was flung over his head. Sammy gasped. Now even if the fog lifted a little, no one would be able to see him – he was just a lump under the blanket, between the man and the horse's head.

A sob tore Sammy's throat. What was happening to poor Mutsy? He could not bear the thought that Mutsy might be dead. He must be alive, he told himself.

If the dog were still alive, could he find Sammy? If he were walking, or the man just dragged him along the road; that would have been all right. Mutsy had a wonderful nose and Alfie had often played a game where Tom or Jack took Sammy out and Alfie released Mutsy five minutes later. The big dog never failed to track him down. That's probably what he had done today – he had tracked Sammy to the Montgomery house and then run upstairs to join him once he began to sing. At the thought of the faithfulness of the poor dog, Sammy felt the tears welling up in his eyes and dripping down his cheeks. His throat swelled and the wire became almost more than he could endure.

Mutsy would track him. If he were still alive,

Mutsy would find him. Mutsy would kill this man; there was no doubt about that. He would kill him like a rat; seize hold of his throat and hold on until he was dead. Sammy concentrated again on the picture of Mutsy, getting up, shaking his poor sore head, and then putting his nose to the ground. Sammy cautiously moved his arm and shook his wrist so that his bleeding fingers were held free of the horse's body. He had to make sure that he laid the trail for Mutsy to follow and that his blood would go drop by drop all along the pavement of Monmouth Street.

And now the horse turned, turned to the left. Sammy curled and uncurled his fingers frantically to keep the blood flowing. His fingertips were wet, but was there enough blood to leave a trail?

This was Long Acre. He could recognise the smell from the coachmaker shops that lined it – a smell of leather and polish and the sharp hot smell of melted metal from the yards behind the shops. Their cellar was near here. If only he didn't have that wire around his throat. If only he could shout. Most of the people living around here – even those who worked in these posh shops – they all knew 'blind Sammy'.

Frantically he struggled, but it was no good. The man gave a sudden hard jerk to the wire and Sammy felt dizzy and sick. He was near death, he knew, and he forced himself to relax his throat so that more air could get in.

Another turn. To the right, this time. Now Sammy was feeling a little better. He managed to get his two hands together. With the nails of his left hand he tore unmercifully at the open cuts on the fingers of his right hand. The blood flowed again and he managed to smear it over the handkerchief that Alfie had tucked into his pocket that morning . . . Would it work? The streets were wet and dirty and the smell of horse manure was overpowering. It seemed impossible that Mutsy should be able to follow him, but Sammy had confidence in his dog.

'He seems to know if you've just passed down a street,' Alfie had reported once. 'Half the time, he doesn't even sniff the ground. He just tears along.'

Corners were the most important places, though. He had to show Mutsy that he had turned. Where was the man taking him? He was definitely turning the horse. They must be turning on to Drury Lane now. Sammy let the bloodstained handkerchief drop from his fingers. If Mutsy were still alive he might follow the clue.

Drury Lane was full of people. Sammy could hear the voices – ordinary voices, complaining of the fog, talking about shopping, greeting each other, making jokes. He relaxed a little. Nothing would happen to him here. He risked slipping his left hand back underneath the rug. The grip on his neck had relaxed a little. Cautiously he inserted first one finger, then another, then another until he had three fingers between the skin of his neck and the sharp biting surface of the wire. If it were tightened now, he could resist for a while.

And now they must be at the entrance to Russell Street. Sammy could smell the stench from the poor people's burying ground at Drury Lane where the bodies were squashed in, one on top of the other. He tried not to flinch from the smell. Every movement he made brought a tightening jerk on the noose.

They were going down the steep hill now. If he had not been held so firmly by the wire around his neck, Sammy would have tumbled over the horse's head. They must be going into the Strand, he thought. This puzzled him. The Strand was always full of people. He could hear the hum as they approached. There were the shouts of the men selling hot pies, the noisy clopping of the horses' hooves, the shrill, high voices of the newspaper sellers and once again the high-pitched squeal of a policeman's whistle. Would the man turn left and go up the Strand towards St Paul's Cathedral, or would he go in the opposite direction towards Charing Cross?

But he did neither. He waited for a while, his horse at a standstill. Sammy's heart beat fast. Perhaps the man was going to let him go. He would never dare to drop a dead body here, right under the noses of the crowd and of the police themselves; if he let him go, he would let him go alive. He hardly dared hope, but yet he did hope.

But no, they were moving again, crossing the Strand. The horse was going a little faster now – crossing the road, obviously. For a moment Sammy still hoped that he would be allowed to slip down from the horse, but then the noose around his neck was jerked cruelly tight. If he had not had his fingers there, he would certainly have choked.

They were going downhill again. Not down a slope, though – these were steps. Wide, shallow steps, thought Sammy, feeling the horse's cautious movements.

And then Sammy's heart suddenly stopped. Even from beneath the blanket, he smelled something new. It was the river. No one could mistake that smell of sewage mixed with a faint saltiness. They were going down the Temple Steps towards the River Thames.

He felt the noose tighten agonisingly, biting almost to the bone of his three fingers. Just before he lost consciousness, he realised what was going to happen.

Now Sammy knew how this man was going to commit his second murder.

CHAPTER 14

ALFIE INVESTIGATES

Alfie walked away briskly after leaving Sammy at the Montgomery household in Bedford Square. On his way out, Sarah had introduced him to the men that worked in mews behind the Montgomery house, and he was planning to come back a little later to see if he could engage the groom or the coachman in conversation. He could always offer to do a few small jobs like cleaning the mud from the wheels of the carriage or brushing out the stables or polishing the leather harness.

First of all he went back to the cellar in Bow Street. There was work to be done and orders to be given if he were to earn the money the inspector had half-promised and keep a roof over all their heads. His mind was churning with tasks to be done, people to see, possibilities to investigate.

'Jack, old son, would you fancy hanging around the betting clubs in Leicester Square? I'd like to know which one of them that Denis Montgomery goes to.'

Jack nodded. He didn't argue, though Alfie knew that Jack, being rather shy, didn't like doing that sort of thing. He much preferred jobs like hunting for coal along the riverside after the barges had been unloaded, or bringing home rotten wood from empty, tumbledown buildings on the quays, or doing some chopping for a friendly butcher in Russell Street.

'I'll go, too,' said Tom.

'No, you won't. You can take Mutsy and do a few tricks with him. We could do with getting in some more money.'

'I don't want to.' Tom was in one of his difficult, whiny moods. Alfie always thought that his mother had spoilt Tom. She had regarded him as a poor motherless babe and had seemed to give him more affection than she gave to her own two sons.

'No, you won't,' he repeated. 'You like eating, don't you? Well, sausages cost money and money don't grow on no trees around here – not that I've noticed, anyways. Listen to the church clock at St Martin-in-the-Fields, and when it's four o'clock, then you go and collect Sammy from the Montgomery place. Number one, Bedford Square – and make sure you go around the back.'

Alfie lurked for a while until Tom and Jack had turned down Long Acre, then he followed them at a distance. He wanted to make sure that Tom followed his orders. It was time that he pulled his weight. He was older than Sammy, but Sammy worked twice as hard as Tom did. Also, he wanted to make sure that Tom didn't take his bad humour out on Mutsy.

The two brothers stopped at the end of Long Acre and Alfie could hear Tom's voice.

'I'll just come with you,' he was saying. 'I'd like to

see inside these gambling clubs.'

'Best do what Alfie tells you.' Jack, as always, was calm.

'I'm sick of Alfie's bossing!'

'He keeps us all fed and out of the streets, don't he?' Jack for once sounded impatient and even angry with his brother. He strode off without another word.

Alfie waited until Tom found a good spot on the corner of Shaftesbury Avenue and watched as he and Mutsy began doing the tricks that Alfie had practised again and again on the dark evenings in their cellar. Tom had Mutsy's big paws in his own two hands and was dancing around singing in his loud, hoarse voice:

'A ring, a ring of roses,
A pocket full of posies,
Atishoo, Atishoo,
All fall down.'

When Tom said 'Atishoo', Mutsy sneezed. That was a trick that Alfie had taught him by tickling his nose with a feather and saying 'Atishoo'. Soon Mutsy would sneeze as soon as anyone said 'Atishoo'.

And then when Tom said 'All fall down', both he

and Mutsy fell to the ground. The weather was bad, but the few shoppers stopped and watched. One lady sent her servant to bring two children from a carriage waiting further down the road. As Alfie passed, he heard a chink of coins in the tin basin. There would not be as good a collection as when Sammy sang, but there might be enough to get supper that night.

Alfie moved away and turned down Monmouth Street. He had decided that his first task was to see Betty. The chances were that she may have been the last person to see Mr Montgomery alive – the last person, that was, except for the murderer.

Betty and her old grandmother lived in a cellar halfway down the street. Betty begged old clothes from the posh houses in Bloomsbury and then she and her grandmother mended them and sold them in the market at Cheapside.

Alfie had become friendly with Betty about a year ago. A well-dressed, drunken man had been pestering her. He had his arm in a deadlock around her neck when Alfie and Mutsy came round the corner from Neal Street. Alfie had instantly given the command, 'Get him, boy' to Mutsy, and Mutsy had seized the man by the seat of his trousers and knocked him to the ground. All three of them fled instantly, Mutsy triumphantly carrying a large piece of good-quality black woollen material in his mouth. Alfie and Mutsy had to lie low for a day or two, but he hadn't regretted doing it.

'If there's anything I can ever do for you,' Betty had said, 'just ask.'

However, when Alfie came to the cellar in Monmouth Street, there was no answer to his knock. He knocked again, but still there was no sound. The one tiny window was firmly shut, but that was not surprising as damp swirls of fog were everywhere and no one wanted it in their rooms. What was strange, though, was there was no sign of candlelight from the window. On a day like this when the fog made the morning as dark as evening, Betts and her grand-mother would definitely need a candle to do the odd bits of sewing that made the old clothes fit to be sold to the market stallholders.

'No one there.' The voice came from the steps next door. The knocking had roused George from the cellar next door. He called himself a shoemaker, but his work consisted in taking old shoes – stolen, or begged from houses in nearby Bloomsbury – and polishing them up and mending holes, sometimes with just a piece of strong cardboard, then selling them on. Most of the people who lived in Monmouth Street were engaged in this business of providing footwear and clothing for poor people and making a few shillings for themselves while they were doing it.

'Where have they gone, George?' Alfie kept his voice polite. George was a strange fellow, liable to go into fits of rage if anyone contradicted him.

'And you ain't the first to be looking for Betty this morning . . . and yesterday, too.' As usual George didn't bother answering the question.

'Oh well, I'd better be off then,' said Alfie cheerfully. He didn't look at George again, but went quickly back up the steps, whistling a little tune as he went. When he reached the railings above George's cellar, he stopped and bent down and pretended to take a splinter of wood from the heel of his bare foot.

'You need a pair of shoes.' George couldn't resist trying for a sale.

'How could I afford a pair of shoes?' Alfie inspected

his heel carefully and then rubbed it.

'Get you a perfect pair for a tanner. Can't say better than that.'

Alfie made a show of turning out his trouser pockets and showing that they were empty. He didn't think he'd get much of a pair of shoes for sixpence. They would fall apart after a few days. George was known to take shoes that were wafer-thin and paint glue over them to give them the strong, shiny appearance of brand new leather. However, he knew that George was bursting with information, and he had to keep him in good humour.

'I'm hoping to get a job soon,' he said. 'Betty was going to talk to a geezer called Mr Montgomery from Bedford Square, about me helping with his horses. Might be able to buy a pair of shoes then.'

George laughed hoarsely. 'You're a slow boy. That Montgomery gent was croaked —' George mimed being choked with a wire '— the night before last, just across the road from here – and guess what? The peelers are looking for Betty. They think that she did it. She was with him that night. I saw her myself.'

And I suppose told the police, too, thought Alfie.

'She in jail now then, is she?' He said the words as if he didn't care.

'Nah, she hopped it. Gone out of London, probably. The grandmother is from the country. Up Hampstead way.'

'No hope of a job for me, then.' Now Alfie just wanted to be on his way. With a quick wave of his hand to George, he moved on briskly, down Monmouth Street towards Seven Dials.

St Giles, that's where I'll look, thought Alfie as he went along the crowded street. Betty would have had more sense than to go to her grandmother's home village. The police would pick her up easily there – everyone knew that the country was the wrong place to go if you wanted to get lost. St Giles was a different matter. It was a well-known fact that if a policeman at St Giles asked a question he would get forty different replies and not a single one of them would be right. By instinct, no one there ever gave a truthful answer to the police.

St Giles was its usual noisy self when Alfie came into the crowded rookeries. He sauntered along for a while – it was a good idea to let the inhabitants have a look at you before venturing any questions.

'Betty, from Monmouth Street,' he said eventually to a woman rescuing her son from a stinking pool of water that had suddenly bubbled up at the centre of one of the courts.

She gave him a long look, taking in his tousled hair, bare feet and shabby clothes, and then nodded in the direction of a tall, falling-down house just behind him.

No more was said, and Alfie did not even acknowledge the information. He strolled over towards the house and climbed the rickety stairs. He had to walk carefully and lightly on the badly sloping staircase, holding on firmly to the banisters.

At the first landing he met a man, wide-eyed and drunken, stumbling down the stairs.

'Betty, the clothes girl from Monmouth Street,' Alfie said briefly. The man hiccoughed and gazed at him with widely open eyes. There was a terrible smell from him, worse than the smell from the privy.

'Plump little girl, about seventeen, curly hair,' added Alfie when there was no reply.

'Where is she?' asked the man. His voice was hoarse

and thick with alcohol. Alfie ignored the question and looked around to see if there was anyone sober who might give him information.

But then the man seized him by the arm. 'Who are you?' he screamed. 'Oh my eyes and ears, what devil's spawn are you? Oh my lungs and liver, I'll rip you open! I'll tear you from limb to limb.'

Crazy, thought Alfie. His heart was thumping, but he had spent the years since his parents died making sure that his feelings did not show on his face, and he looked at the mad man with what he knew would be a calm, indifferent expression. It seemed to work, as after a minute the man dropped his arm and went clumping down the stairs.

'You looking for a girl?' An old woman popped out of a door on the landing. Alfie swallowed twice. He didn't trust his voice, so he just nodded.

'You haven't heard, then?'

He shook his head.

'A girl fell through the rotten boards in the privy last night. She fell into the cesspool below. She was drowned when they fished her out.'

CHAPTER 15

THE CRUMBLING HOUSE

Alfie looked around the crumbling house, with the crazily leaning staircase, the chunks of rotten plaster dangling from the walls, the broken windows and the missing floorboards. He shuddered. He had been fond of Betty. She had been kind to the boys from time to time – whenever she had some luck herself.

He returned down the stairs, feeling his heart skip a beat every time that the wood creaked beneath his bare feet. He knew where the privy was: the smell was unmistakable. When he reached the bottom step he stared down the dimly lit back passageway. The door was askew, swinging on its hinges and, beyond it, from the faint sheen, he guessed that what was left of the floor was underwater. He turned his face aside at the stench – the smell from the privy in his own place was bad enough, but this was unbearable.

'Don't go in there,' he yelled as a little girl of about four, filthy, and dressed in what looked like the moth-eaten top-half of a woman's frock, approached the door and stood hesitating on the threshold, peering in at the flooded floor. 'Go out in the street,' he said, trying to sound like someone in authority. If she went in, he was afraid that he would not have the courage to rescue her.

She looked startled at his shout, burst into tears, but turned and ran out into the street. Alfie heaved a sigh of relief and began to follow her, still treading carefully. It looked to him as if the whole house had lurched to one side.

He had only taken a step when he saw a door open slightly and then close again. It was enough, though.

He had caught a glimpse of a woman's boa, its originally white feathers filthy and bedraggled. He knew who always wrapped her throat in that thing.

Alfie didn't hesitate. Immediately he knocked on the door. There was no reply, but he knocked again. 'It's just Alfie, Alfie from Bow Street,' he whispered in through the keyhole.

There was still no reply, but he sensed that someone was there and waited patiently. A minute later, he heard the sound of the bolt being drawn back, and there was Betty.

'What do you want?' she asked in a whisper. Her usually pink cheeks were the colour of chalk and her large blue eyes had heavy shadows under them.

Alfie did not hesitate. In a second he was through the door and shutting it firmly behind him.

'You all right, Betts?' he asked.

She shivered, turning even paler, and her eyes looked even bigger than usual.

'I didn't kill him, Alfie,' she said in a whisper.

'Course you didn't.' He made his voice sound reassuring. He didn't think she had – she didn't have the nerve. And why should she? Mr Montgomery was worth more alive than dead to Betty. Anyway, *if* she had garrotted him, she wouldn't have missed the watch.

'What time was it when you left him?' he asked quickly.

'The bell was being rung at St Giles church,' she said after a minute's thought. If she had answered more quickly, Alfie would have guessed that it was a planned answer, but now he was inclined to think she had answered truthfully. About nine o'clock, then – that was the last service of the day. The body must have lain in the doorway until the police found it there the following morning. That end of Monmouth Street was St Giles territory, and the people of St Giles minded their own business about murder as well as everything else.

'And which way did he go? Back towards Bedford Square?'

She frowned and then said, 'No, he went the other way, down towards Long Acre.'

'And?' Alfie could see from her expression that she was holding something back.

'And nothing.'

112

'Go on, Betts, tell me! You can't stay hidden here for ever. Once the murderer is caught you can go back to Monmouth Street.' Betty looked unconvinced so Alfie added, 'I've got a few ideas of my own, so who knows, I might be able to catch the fellow that did it. Then you'll be in the clear, won't you?'

She smiled then, and a little colour came back to her cheeks. '*You* find the murderer?' she said incredulously.

Alfie nodded. 'See someone follow him, did you?' He made his voice sound firm and assured.

Betty nodded. 'Fellow passed me,' she said hesitantly.

'Notice anything about him?'

Betty thought for a moment. 'He had a funny smell from him,' she said unexpectedly.

'A smell!' Alfie was used to smells. You didn't smell yourself normally, but sometimes you smelled other people. That drunken man coming down the stairs had smelled so bad that Alfie had held his breath until he passed.

'Not a toff, then,' he said after a minute. Toffs didn't smell. Toffs had servants to boil up water for them and lug up buckets of it to their bedrooms. Some of them even had special washing places called bathrooms. Alfie

113

was disappointed that it was not a toff that Betty had seen following Mr Montgomery. If one of the residents of St Giles had killed Mr Montgomery it would be as much as his life was worth to breathe a hint of it to the police. But then there was the evidence of the turned-out pockets and the watch still sitting in its fob. Alfie still felt sure that it was a toff that murdered Mr Montgomery.

Sure enough, Betty was shaking her head. 'He was a toff, all right,' she said. 'It wasn't a bad smell. Just a kind of sharp smell.'

'Like tobacco?'

Betty shook her head again. 'No, a funny smell. I've never smelled it before.'

Alfie pushed the discussion about smells to the back of his mind. Betts wasn't too bright – she wouldn't be able to describe the smell any better. Perhaps it was just some kind of soap – or perhaps some of that perfumed stuff that barbers rubbed in men's beards.

'And he followed Mr Montgomery?'

Betty nodded. 'Just behind him.'

'Montgomery was garrotted with a wire, you

know,' said Alfie, glad of the chance to show off his knowledge. 'Was this fellow near enough to do that?'

'Could be . . .' Betty sounded dubious and then said quickly, 'I remember now – I thought he was going to tap him on the shoulder. I couldn't tell you what he looked like, though.' She paused and added with a shudder, 'He was just a shadow, really. A giant black shadow with a big tall hat.'

CHAPTER 16

THE GATEKEEPER'S SLATE

'Going to be a terrible evening when the fog is as bad as this at noon.' Determined to impress the good-natured coachman, Alfie scrubbed vigorously at the wheels of the coach in the warmth of the stable behind number one, Bedford Square.

The elderly coachman rubbed his gnarled old hands, threw his cape over his shoulders, peered out of the stable and then came back quickly. He had a look of Alfie's grandfather about his face, and Alfie suddenly felt quite at home with him.

'A real pea-souper of a fog – that's what we're going to have, mate. What they call a London particular. Here, have some of that beer and bread and cheese. Cold day out there! So you're a friend of Sarah. Nice little girl, that.'

'I suppose you're hoping you don't have to go out in that fog this evening.' Alfie took a big bite from the bread and cheese and looked innocently at the coachman.

'This coach hasn't been out for days,' said the coachman hoarsely. 'Just as well with the cough that I've had on my chest for the last week.'

'Ladies don't like the fog,' said Alfie knowledgeably. 'I suppose the two gents just take their horses when they go out.'

'Not even that.' The coachman gave a glance over at the riding horses munching at their hay basket. 'These fellows over there haven't been out for three days. I was saying to John here this morning,' he looked over at the groom, who was rubbing some saddles, 'we'll just have to take them out tomorrow, even if it is only to walk them around the square. They'll be getting restless and bad-tempered otherwise.'

'So will the gentlemen if they're shut up in the house for days on end!' Alfie wanted to keep the coachman's mind on Denis Montgomery and Mr Scott. And what about the butler? Dare he ask if the butler had gone out on Monday night?

'Well, there's been a tragedy in the family. Have you heard about that?' John the groom came to join them. 'Pity Mr Montgomery wasn't on his horse on Monday night – he might still be with us if he were.'

Alfie took a long swallow of the beer. It was good stuff, much better than he could ever afford to buy for himself.

'That's right,' agreed the coachman.

'Of course, the master wouldn't want a horse, anyway.' John nudged the coachman and Alfie pretended not to see. He guessed that they knew Mr Montgomery was going to see Betty. They probably sniggered about their master and the girl from Monmouth Street. 'And Mr Denis was probably just going to the gaming club in Leicester Square, or else that new one at Piccadilly Circus – The Royal Saloon, it's called, I think. He wouldn't take a horse there. Sometimes he takes a cab and sometimes he walks. I think that Mr Scott went with him.'

'Well, I'd better be getting along.' Alfie got to his feet and drained the last drops from his pewter mug.

'Take what's left of that jug of beer over to the gatekeeper, will you?' said the coachman. 'Poor soul, he must be frozen there, and no one thinks of him. He don't belong to any of the houses. Tell him to drop back the jug some time.'

'You'll remember me if ever you think of taking on a boy in the stables, will you?' asked Alfie, accepting the jug. 'I'll drop by from time to time and see if you have any news for me.' It was just as well to go now, before he roused any suspicions by asking too many questions. In any case, thought Alfie as he went out into the fog, he had got a fair amount of information. So Mr Denis Montgomery had gone out on that Monday night – and gone out on foot. It was a nuisance that it appeared as if Mr Scott had gone with him. Strange, that . . . After all, he was Mr Montgomery's partner in the Indian tea business, so why did he go out with the son, not with the father?

Quickly, Alfie went back up Bedford Avenue, which housed the mews, turned to the right and made his way towards the huge twenty-foot gates that kept the inhabitants of Bedford Square secure from the outside world and from people like the inhabitants of St Giles.

'Here's some beer from the coachman at number one.' The gift was accepted, but the gatekeeper didn't seem interested in talking and had turned his back when Alfie said pleadingly, 'Could I have a warm by your fire, mister?' Despite the warming beer and cheese in his stomach, he was freezing. The damp cold was seeping into his clothes and his hair felt wringing wet.

The gatekeeper nodded.

'Hard job you have here in all weathers!' Alfie said sympathetically.

'Hard enough,' agreed the man, poking his fire and throwing on a few more coals.

'Boring too, innit? I bet you hardly know who goes in or out during the day and the night. You must be so used to them.'

'I notice all right. It makes it less boring.' The gate-keeper looked at Alfie, as if wondering whether to trust him, and then gave a sudden grin. He turned to the cupboard behind him and took something out. 'Look here on this little bit of slate! Sometimes I make a guess where they are going and then I make a guess when they'll be back. I write down when they go out and put my guess here, and then if they come within half an hour of my guess I win, and if I'm more than half an hour out then they win. Wait a minute.'

The gatekeeper nipped out and opened the gate, bowing politely and touching his hat as a stout man on a horse rode out, followed by a groom on foot.

'That's number eighteen. He'll be back at one o'clock for his lunch – that's what I'd guess.'

The gatekeeper made a note on the slate. Alfie looked over his shoulder. He wished he could read.

'What have you there?' he asked.

'Mr M. from number one,' read the gatekeeper. 'Well, he went out on Monday night, and he never came back,' he said. 'That's one that I lost. And look here, Mr D. M. from number one, that's Mr Denis Montgomery. I won that one. Back in two hours.

And there's R.M. from number one.'

'Who's Are Em?' Alfie had never heard of a name like that.

'Don't you even know your alphabet?' asked the gatekeeper. 'Well, R is for red and M is for mouth, and I call him that because he has a red mouth. I saw him once going out the gate, and he yawned in my face. Gave me a shock, it did. He had a mouth like the devil, all bright red, tongue and all.'

'And you lost on that one?' Alfie was beginning to distinguish between the ticks and the crosses.

'That's right. You're getting the hang of it now. I put him down for the same time as Mr Denis – they went out together, but they didn't come back together. The visitor didn't come back until nearly midnight. That surprised me. He came back just before I locked the gate – of course, he could have come in by this little gate at the side, being as he was on foot. And Mr Denis came back at his usual time, about one o' clock in the morning.'

And then a shadow of a tall man in an overcoat and a top hat fell across the entrance to the cosy little hut of the gatekeeper.

'What's that boy doing there?' asked a voice. 'Get rid of him, Thompson. This is not a hideaway for street brats.'

'That's the butler from the Montgomery place,' the gatekeeper whispered into Alfie's ear as the man left. 'You'd better go now.'

Alfie went rapidly out with barely a glance at the butler. He was tall and strong-looking, but it was his voice that impressed Alfie. It was the voice of a man used to power, a man used to bullying those beneath him, but also it was the angry, irritable voice of a man who was worried. Alfie wondered whether Sammy would have an opportunity to listen to the butler. Once again he thought of his blind brother in that house where a murderer probably lurked. Had he done the right thing in allowing Sammy to go there? There were times when Alfie wished he could just be a child and not have to keep deciding everything, but he pushed the thought away. It was stupid to look back – he was the oldest, and he had to take the responsibility.

Once he was through the gate, he lingered for a moment and then slipped back. The butler had not stopped to talk to the gatekeeper. He was making his way towards Bloomsbury Street. So why had he come up to the gate?

Strange place to live, thought Alfie looking through the tall, black railings at the square: those solid blocks of houses ranged around three sides, all with windows heavily screened with lace curtains, the small garden in the middle, those heavy iron gates blocking out the ordinary people, a place where no one would commit a crime for fear of the unseen eyes watching through those windows.

But, of course, there were Monmouth Street and St Giles, both so near, and yet so far . . .

Was the criminal hiding there?

Or sitting at ease in this place that smelled of money, power and privilege?

Alfie went on his way thoughtfully, his mind churning with the information that he had uncovered.

Where did Denis Montgomery go on the night that his father was murdered?

Why did Mr Scott come back before him? And what did Mr Scott, a stranger to London, find to do until midnight that night?

What did the butler have to hide?

And why did he find a boy talking to the gate-keeper so threatening?

CHAPTER 17

THE MASKED GAMBLERS

The cellar seemed warm and almost bright when Alfie came in from the cold, damp fog. The fire was glowing – thanks to Jack they always had plenty of coal, as he scoured the river's edge every morning and often dragged home a sackful when the bargemen had been extra careless in loading the carts.

Mallesh was sitting by the fire and beside him was Tom. While Mutsy was greeting Alfie with his usual tail-wagging excitement, Mallesh went on telling Tom about the Grand Trunk Road in India. It had four lines of shade-giving trees, he was saying. The English officers in scarlet coats rode their horses down the central strip, the Indians walked or travelled in heavy carts along the side strips and there were *caravanserais* where travellers could sleep overnight.

'You must have done well, Tom. You're back early. Got the money for supper, have you? And something for the extra rent?' Alfie tried to keep his temper down until he heard the facts.

'What, in weather like this?' Tom made the mistake of sniggering. It was to impress Mallesh, Alfie knew, but he was in no mood to be indulgent to Tom. It was essential that this murder were solved quickly, and solved by Alfie. Otherwise, if this fog and bad weather went on for months and the begging money dried up, they would be thrown out of their cellar, and then what would happen?

'How much?' The tone of Alfie's voice warned Tom, who mutely emptied his pockets, scattering the coins on the box that they used as a table.

'Three pence halfpenny! And you came home with that!'

'I was wet and cold,' said Tom sullenly.

'And the rest of us go dry and warm, I suppose.' Alfie stuck his fists in his pockets and did his best to keep his temper.

'Sammy is. It's not fair. He gets all the best jobs – just because he's your brother. Why do we all have to work to keep him?'

'Get out! Go on, get out!' Alfie's patience broke and he gave Tom a box on the ear. 'Get out there and try at least to get another few pence. Don't forget to go for Sammy at four. Mutsy, go with Tom, good boy, Mutsy.'

'Could I help? Do something?' Mallesh looked anxious as the boy and the dog retreated silently.

'No, you stay put. It's not going to help having you in jail. Stay put and think hard about why someone should murder Mr Montgomery. Who knows, it might be something to do with India after all. I'm going to look for Jack at Leicester Square.'

This time he did not bother following Tom, who had turned down Drury Lane, but struck out towards

Leicester Square. He was anxious about Jack. Jack was a good fellow, but he was useless at telling lies. Alfie was worried in case Jack had got into trouble in the betting clubs.

There was no sign of Jack in Leicester Square. Alfie patiently went from club to club, and then up a couple of the side streets.

Alfie was almost going to give up the hunt when he spotted Jack coming out from the cellar of one of the most low-down clubs in Leicester Square. Not the sort of place that Denis Montgomery would have gone to, thought Alfie.

Jack was white-faced and stank of beer and spirits. He shook his head as Alfie approached.

'Afraid I haven't found anything out,' he said in a low voice. 'The fellows that gave me jobs taking out bottles didn't know anything much about the toffs that go to the clubs. I got seven pence, though.'

'Great,' said Alfie. 'That will do for supper.' He always liked to have something for his gang every night. It kept the spirits high. 'You go home; you look a bit done in. I'll just have a poke around and then I'll follow you.'

Jack hesitated. 'Be careful,' he said after a minute. 'There's some queer people around these clubs. Chances are I've done enough questioning. They might turn nasty.'

'Tell you what,' said Alfie. 'I'll leave these ones in Leicester Square. I'll just go on down to Piccadilly Circus and look for one called The Royal Saloon. The fellow who works with the Montgomery horses told me about that one.'

Jack nodded and went off, walking wearily, his head hanging and his shoulders slumped.

It was no wonder that Jack had looked so exhausted, thought Alfie half an hour later. On the instructions of the porter, he had gone up and down the back stairs of The Royal Saloon time after time, collecting bottles, bringing them down to the cellar, washing them out and then stacking them so that they could be sold back to the beer and wine merchants. The crates were very heavy and the stairs were steep; he had been told to make no noise, as the customers were playing cards or tossing dice behind the door on the landing. Eventually, just as he was about to turn to go down the stairs, he felt a bottle slide and lodge underneath his foot, then he overbalanced, and, desperately clutching the crate to his chest, slipped and bumped down to the bottom.

'What's that noise?' A man appeared through the baize-lined door, shutting it carefully after him.

'Oh my God, that's the steward. Now we're in trouble,' whispered the porter. Quickly he grabbed the crate of bottles from Alfie and disappeared on down to the cellar.

'Nothing broken, just one unlucky fellow.' Alfie dragged himself to his feet and stretched his arms and legs, patting himself all over as if to check for damage. Luckily there had been a carpet – probably to prevent noise – and he didn't think that he was too badly hurt. He managed a jolly expression.

The steward gave a grin. 'Well, you're a plucky youngster,' he said. 'Good job nobody from up there saw you fall. They'd all have been putting bets on whether you would be killed or not.'

'You're joking me!' Alfie could tell that this was a bored man who liked to chat. He saw his chance to get some useful information.

'I'm not! Do you know, about a year ago, a man who came in here and gambled every night of the year with his friends fell down on the doorstep when he was going home, and guess what his friends did?'

'Called a cab?' asked Alfie with his most innocent expression.

'Nah, they all started to bet on whether he was dead or just had a fit! I got the porter to run and get a surgeon and you'll never guess what happened when the surgeon arrived . . .'

'What?' asked Alfie, all eager attention.

'They told me to send him away – that it would spoil the bet.' The steward laughed heartily and Alfie joined in.

'Well, I bet they are a crowd of freaks! I suppose you know them all,' Alfie said after a few seconds. 'There was a gent who got himself garrotted up near where I live. A Mr Montgomery from India. Someone said that he was a great one for gaming houses.'

'Didn't come here.' The steward was quite definite. 'I know who you mean, though. Read about it in today's paper. I'll tell you something, though – his son was here that night.'

'Not with his father, then – on his own?'

'I think that he brought a guest with him – can't remember too well, but I have that impression. Yes, he did. I remember now. He said that this fellow was visiting from India. They didn't take too many chips, though, so one or other of them were not planning to stay too long.' The steward paused. 'Come on, do you want to have a look inside? You can see them all – mad they are, every one of them! Just put on this apron – it will cover your clothes. Take this crate in your hands and you can take out some of the empty bottles for me.'

Alfie slid in cautiously and had a quick look around. To his immense astonishment, over half of the gentlemen seemed to be wearing masks – so that no one could tell from their expressions if they were betting on a certainty or a wild card, according to a whisper from the steward. Was the Monmouth Street strangler sitting there, playing cards, and watching Alfie from behind his mask with cold, cruel eyes? He was glad to get out – he didn't like the thought of being watched by a possible murderer, when he himself could see very few faces at all.

He went on down to the cellar with the bottles, received a grudging two pence from the porter and then, saying he was too sore and stiff to do any more, he slipped out of the back door to the club house.

Well, he thought as he went on his way, Denis Montgomery and Mr Scott did go to the Royal Saloon that night, and one of them probably left early – the gatekeeper had said that Mr Scott was late home, so he probably went to some other place in the West End. But Mr Montgomery was murdered early in the evening – about nine o'clock if Betty was right. The chances were that the murderer would have gone straight back to Bedford Square, rather than hang around the streets to be arrested by the police . . .

Alfie was halfway up a small deserted lane leading out of Leicester Square, deep in thought, when he heard a shrill cry of, 'Alfie, look behind you!' He wheeled around. The lane was dimly lit and the fog was very thick, but some lights spilled out of a shop window and on to the road.

And there, just behind him, he saw an immense

black shadow: a shadow of a man, whose top hat and raised cudgel were outlined on the cobbled street.

CHAPTER 18

WHERE'S SAMMY?

A brick hurtled through the air and crashed down to the ground. The man wheeled around; Jack shouted again, and Alfie ran for it. He knew these alleyways like the back of his hand. He turned off to the left and ran as fast as he could, trying to ignore the fierce pain across his lower ribs. There was a thundering noise in his ears as he tried to gulp in more air. He had a strong urge to keep running all the way back to the cellar, but he had to see that Jack was safe, so he turned again until he was in a narrow alley leading back towards the lane – and then there was Jack, running towards him.

'Did you see his face?' Alfie just managed to gulp out the words.

Jack shook his head. 'Nah, his back was to me. Didn't half give me a fright, though. I thought you was a goner for a minute.'

'Good thing you're handy with a brick.' To his horror Alfie felt a rush of sour liquid fill his mouth. He felt himself start to heave, and drew in a long breath. He didn't want to stand vomiting in the street here if the strangler was after him.

'Let's scarper!' Jack was practical as ever. He put an arm around his cousin's shoulders and steered him back into the alleyway. 'We'll just go nice and quietly along here,' he said. 'We'll keep our eyes peeled and walk near the doorways. If he comes back we'll see him before he sees us.'

Alfie nodded silently. For once Jack was taking the lead, but he was happy to say nothing. He still felt sick and his legs were unsteady.

'We'll be home before you know it,' said Jack after a few minutes, and Alfie nodded again.

Up to this hour it had been almost a game, but now Alfie was frightened. Why, he asked himself again, had he allowed his blind brother to go into a house where a murderer might live?

By now the fog was so thick that even the candles in the windows of the houses were nothing but faint blobs of misty light. The gas lamps of Monmouth Street fizzed gently in the wet air but gave little light.

'Where's Sammy?' As soon as Alfie opened the door to the underground cellar he knew that something was wrong. Tom was there, chatting to Mallesh, but there was no Mutsy to come bounding up to greet them and Sammy's fireside chair was empty.

'We were wondering that ourselves,' said Tom. He sounded a little guilty. 'Mutsy took off. He went too fast for me to follow, but I reckoned he had gone to Bedford Square. We reckoned that Sammy must have waited for Sarah. Here she comes now. That's her on the stairs, I reckon.'

Alfie dashed back to the door and threw it open.

'Sarah, where's Sammy?' He could hear the terror in his voice.

'What?' Sarah's voice rose high with alarm. 'He's not home yet? But he must be! He left ages ago. He and Mutsy together!'

'Why didn't you go for Sammy, Tom?' Alfie tried hard to keep his temper – more for Jack's sake than for Tom's. Jack had saved his life.

'Like I said, Mutsy took off.' Tom gave a careless shrug of his shoulders. 'I reckoned that he would go to Bedford Square and fetch Sammy home.'

'Mutsy came to the house all right.' Sarah was almost breathless. 'He burst in when Sammy was singing and the missus said that Sammy could go an hour early. They went off together more than an hour ago.'

'More than an hour ago,' breathed Jack. His voice had a frightened sound in it and Alfie felt his heart thumping with quick beats. Bedford Square was only about half a mile away. Sammy should only have taken a quarter of that time to walk it with Mutsy to guide him. He turned to Sarah.

'Where was Sammy all day?'

'In the butler's pantry.'

'And the butler saw him, did he?

'No,' said Sarah. 'The butler was out all morning.'

'That's a lie,' snapped Alfie. His voice was sharp and rough, but Sarah understood the terrible fear that was gripping him and she said nothing. After a moment, he said, 'I saw him – the butler, I mean – near the house. He was there about two o'clock. He was suspicious of me – I could tell by the way that he ordered me away from the gatekeeper. Chances are he might be even more suspicious of Sammy there in the house.'

'We'd better go and look for Sammy.' Jack turned back to the door again.

'I will come with you,' said Mallesh. 'No one will see me in this fog.'

'But what happened to —' Sarah stopped. She had heard something – something on the steps leading down to the cellar.

Something was coming down those steps – not walking, not running, but lurching down, crashing against the walls, something that seemed blind, or drunk, or out of its mind. Something with no eyes, no balance, no brain . . .

And it was coming towards their door.

Alfie snatched up a torch, thrust it into the fire and carried it to the door. Jack was after him in a second. Tom clutched Sarah's hand and Mallesh slid his knife out and brandished it.

And then Alfie flung open the door and cried, 'Mutsy!' and when the dog heard that voice, he made a great effort and staggered on shaking legs down the last two steps, and then he stood trembling violently with his head hanging almost to his knees.

'He's been in the river. He's soaking,' said Jack.

'We can see that, blockhead.' Alfie did not often snap at Jack, but the sight of Mutsy was terrifying him. He was still shaking after his own ordeal and now he seemed plunged into a nightmare where Sammy had disappeared and Mutsy was no longer the protector and guardian of the blind boy.

'He's dripping on to the floor.' Tom's voice was shaking.

'He's injured.' Mallesh put his knife away and looked at the dog with concern. 'That is a very bad cut he has on his head.'

'Bring him over to the fire, Alfie, and let's see

what's wrong with him.' Sarah stuck the poker in the fire and stirred it so that a bright flame lit the room.

'Come on, boy,' said Alfie, snapping his fingers.

For a moment it seemed as if Mutsy could not even hear that simple command. Alfie took hold of the rough rope collar around the dog's neck and tried to drag him, but for the first time in Mutsy's life he defied his master and a long low growl came from him.

'The dog is mad.' Mallesh's dark skin had gone a sickly yellow and his eyes were wide with anxiety.

'No, he isn't.' But there was a dark fear in Alfie's mind. Would Mutsy, if he were in his right mind, have ever left Sammy? Alfie didn't like to think back to the time before Mutsy had brought warmth and fun and security into the little gang of boys in the Bow Street cellar. And what would Sammy do without him?

'Give him a drink of water,' suggested Mallesh. 'If he is mad, he won't drink water.'

'Rabies, you mean,' said Sarah, but she fetched Mutsy's bowl and filled it from the bucket under the sink. Mallesh backed away nervously, but Sarah put the bowl down beside the dog's muzzle without fear.

Mutsy would not hurt any of them; she was sure of that.

And Mutsy drank and drank and drank. It seemed as if he would never stop. And when he lifted his dripping muzzle from the bowl his eyes were clearer. He looked directly at Alfie and Alfie saw something in his gaze that made his heart stop suddenly. He knew that Mutsy was trying to tell him something. He had been blocking the thought from his mind during the last few minutes.

Mutsy turned and began to go back up the steps. His legs seemed steadier now, after the drink of water, and he no longer lurched from side to side.

'Stay here,' said Alfie rapidly to Mallesh. 'Keep the fire going and boil some water, lots of water.' If Sammy were badly hurt, they would need the water to clean his wounds as well as Mutsy's.

But then the thought Alfie had been blocking welled up again. What if Sammy were dead?

CHAPTER 19

STUMBLING THROUGH THE FOG

'Keep together,' snapped Alfie when they were out in Bow Street.

It was easy to keep up with Mutsy; the big dog's legs seemed weak as he plodded heavily along Long Acre and then turned towards Drury Lane. The danger was in getting separated in this fog as dense as yellow cotton-wool.

'Where's he going?' asked Tom from behind him.

His voice was choked. Alfie looked over his shoulder. Sarah and Tom were just behind him and Sarah was holding Tom's arm. Alfie was glad she was there. Tom would be blaming himself for not fetching Sammy as he had been told to do. Once again, Alfie's mind shied away from the thought that had come into it.

'Going to the river, of course, you muffin!' Alfie tried to make his voice sound light. It was up to him to keep his gang in good heart. He forced himself to go on. 'Sammy probably missed his footing and then stumbled in the river and Mutsy went after him and now Mutsy's bringing us to him. Perhaps Sammy hurt his leg or something.'

'But why is Mutsy bleeding? And what were they doing near the river anyways?' Tom's voice was low and hoarse.

'Shut up, Tom,' growled Jack.

Sarah said nothing. Sarah had brains. Alfie knew she would have guessed the situation.

Alfie tried to pray as he followed Mutsy's stumbling body around the corner into Drury Lane. His grandfather had taught him and Sammy a lot of prayers. He wished that he could remember them now. His grandfather had been a religious man. He was from Ireland. He had been very musical too and he was the one who had taught Sammy to play the fiddle and sing so beautifully almost as soon as he could talk. 'Poor child, we must give him the means to earn his living later on,' Alfie could remember him saying.

Well, his grandfather was gone now, dead of fever, and the fiddle was gone, too – sold in a bad time – and Sammy . . .

'Bet Mutsy brings us across the Strand,' said Alfie aloud. He would try to keep talking – it would help to keep his thoughts away from the dreadful possibility of finding Sammy's dead body and it would keep up the spirits of the rest of the gang. He was sorry now that he had shouted at Tom. It was not Tom's fault. He should have gone to fetch Sammy himself, should have kept his brother safe . . .

'Keep near to the shops!' he commanded. There were lots of people on the Strand – all groping their way with outstretched arms, trying to make sure that they did not wander on to the road where the iron-shod feet of the horses clattered along the paving stones.

Alfie was worried about Mutsy. The poor dog was going more and more slowly and his breath sounded noisy. From time to time, he stopped and shook his head; Alfie could hear the big hairy ears flapping, but he always set off again staggering down the road. Alfie slipped his hand through the knotted rope around the dog's neck. He had made this collar himself and had finished it with a big knot so that Sammy could hold on to it and walk securely at the side of his faithful friend.

Now, Alfie had the feeling that it was only his grip on this collar that kept Mutsy from falling to the ground.

'We must be coming near to the Temple Stairs now. Should we cross?' asked Sarah. She had guessed what he had guessed, but Alfie shook his head.

'No, we'll let Mutsy lead us. He's in charge. No point in confusing him.'

'Mutsy will find him.' Tom was beginning to sound better.

'Yes, of course he will. Mutsy can always find

Sammy,' said Sarah. She sounded very sure. Alfie wondered whether she was trying to reassure Tom or whether she really believed it.

And then Mutsy collapsed on the ground. One minute he was staggering along, with Alfie's hand holding the collar, and the next he was a dead weight, just a limp bag of bones. Alfie almost fell on top of the poor fellow.

'Oh no,' sobbed Tom. Alfie heard Sarah gulp. Jack cleared his throat noisily.

In the faint gleam from the stained glass door top of the gas-lit public house beside them, Alfie could see that they were all looking at him, all wondering what to do next. He kneeled down on the wet pavement and looked into Mutsy's eyes. Was the dog dead?

But no, Mutsy's eyes looked back into his and those eyes were full of intelligence, full of shame, too, as if the dog were apologising for his weakness.

Alfie stood up resolutely. 'Keep stroking him, Sarah,' he said, and then he fumbled in the inside pocket of his jacket and took out a penny. Without another glance at Mutsy, he moved away and opened the door and stepped into the warm, beer-smelling pub.

Inside there was a huge crowd of people, all drinking heavily to take the taste of the fog from their mouths.

'A pint of beer,' Alfie said as loudly as he could, once he'd managed to get to the counter. He slapped down a penny on the dirty surface.

'Penny halfpenny,' said the barman, filling a pewter mug from the wooden cask on the counter.

'And a bowl of water for my dog.' Alfie prised out another halfpenny and held it in his hand.

There was no fuss about that. Of course, it was the sort of pub where men often brought their bulldogs and discussed fights and bet on results. The barman took a bowl from under the counter, filled it from a bucket and handed it over.

When he got back outside, all three of them were kneeling on the ground beside Mutsy's still body.

'Oh, Grandad, don't let him die,' whispered Alfie. He meant to pray to God, but it seemed easier to pray to his grandfather. His mother had told him that her father was such a good man that he would have gone straight to Heaven.

Quickly he poured away the water and then carefully tipped the whole mug of beer into the bowl.

'Here, Tom, take that mug back inside,' he said, and then he knelt down beside Mutsy. The dog's eyes were shut, but he was panting.

'Here's a treat for you, old lad,' Alfie said huskily. 'Beer! Mutsy, beer!'

And Mutsy's eyes snapped open quite suddenly. Of all things in the world – after sausages – Mutsy loved beer. With a groan he rolled over on his front. Now Alfie could put the bowl between the dog's front paws. Mutsy's tongue came out and touched the delicious sweet taste. He lapped – one hesitant lap. And then another. And then another.

Then Mutsy dragged himself to his feet. He bent his head and lapped up the whole pint of beer and cleaned the dish afterwards.

And after that he looked at Alfie and his eyes said, *Come on, we've wasted enough time.*

Without hesitation, Alfie kicked the bowl aside. Someone would probably stumble over it in the fog, but he didn't care. The pint of beer would give

Mutsy some energy for a while, but it wouldn't last too long. There was no doubt the poor dog was badly injured.

But Mutsy was going well now, almost trotting, instead of staggering. Down the Strand they went in the eerie whiteness of the fog, which seemed to absorb and dull the lights from the shops, the gas lamps and the cabs.

Then Mutsy suddenly stopped. For a moment, Alfie thought the dog was going to fall again, but Mutsy was just putting his nose to the ground. He sniffed for a moment, then wheeled around and turned to cross the road. He did not hesitate for a moment when they reached the opposite pavement, but went steadily on until they came to the Temple Stairs. His paws slipped a little on the wet stone surface, but Alfie kept a tight grip on his collar and they reached the bottom of the steps in safety. There was no one around. It was dark now and no boat or ship was visible on the Thames – just great swirling masses of fog and a faint gleam of light from Waterloo Bridge.

There were no people around either, no one fishing

for eels in the muddy water, or searching for pieces of coal along the shoreline.

No one at all.

Nothing but a sodden heap of rags at the bottom of the steps.

CHAPTER 20

THE BODY ON THE STEPS

Mutsy collapsed at the bottom of the steps. Then he made a big effort and crawled towards the figure lying there and collapsed again. Alfie dropped to his knees beside the body. In the darkness there was no sure way of telling who it was, but Alfie knew.

However, there was a strong stench of vomit all around, and Mutsy was silent. Alfie tried to tell himself that Sammy was still alive, that he had sicked up the river water and was now unconscious – but only unconscious. If he were dead, Mutsy would definitely have howled. He had even howled when their cat died one night.

Sarah gave a little sobbing gasp and Tom cried out, 'That ain't our Sammy?', but Alfie wasted no time. He fumbled with his hand until he found the curly head and moved down to the forehead, deadly cold. Surely no one could be as cold as that and still be alive.

'Get up those steps as quick as you can, Jack, and bring me that torch from the top of the Temple Steps. Just lift it out and carry it down.' Alfie's voice was fierce and Jack was gone before the last words were out of his mouth.

And then he remembered the doctor who had come to see his mother. He had placed a tiny looking glass over her mouth then shown it to him, saying sadly, 'There's no moisture, is there? She's dead, I'm afraid, sonny.'

Alfie slid his fingers down the face until they covered his brother's mouth. Was there a faint warmth?

His own hands were cold and damp, but he blew on them hard and then tried again. Yes, this time there was something, a breath – or was he just trying to convince himself, the way he tried to convince himself that his mother was not dead on that terrible day two years ago?

'Got the torch.' Jack was beside him, the smell of the pitch tar very strong. These torches were lit every night on the Temple Stairs in case someone fell into the river and light was needed.

And then everything began to happen. The strong tarry smell made Mutsy sneeze. He lifted his head, got to his feet and stood over Sammy with big panting breaths. By the light of the torch Alfie could see the steam of Mutsy's breath coming up from Sammy's white face. His colourless lips were parted. Surely they hadn't been like that before.

From behind him, Alfie heard Sarah draw in a quick breath. She knelt down and took Sammy's hand in between hers and began to rub it.

'Take the other hand, Alfie,' she said urgently. 'Keep rubbing. Tom, you rub his feet. Jack, hold that torch as near as possible – not that near, you numbskull – you'll set us all on fire.' Her voice rose up quite high and then Sammy stirred slightly and moaned and opened his eyes.

'God, I'm cold.' It was just a whisper, but he had spoken.

'Let's get you and poor old Mutsy home,' said Alfie, taking off his worn jacket and wrapping it around Sammy. He wished he could punch someone, or turn a somersault or something. 'Come on, lad, put your arms around my neck and I'll carry you.'

'It was the Monmouth Street strangler,' whispered Sammy. He lifted his chin and by the light of the torch Alfie could see the narrow red wound on his brother's neck.

By the time they had climbed the Temple Stairs and gone up the steep, narrow passageway that led to the Strand, Alfie knew that something had to be done. Despite having Alfie and Jack's jackets around him, Sammy was shivering violently. Mutsy was staggering and sitting down suddenly from time to time.

'Should Jack run home and get the barrow?'

asked Sarah, looking anxiously at Sammy as Jack replaced the torch into its holder.

'Let me think,' said Alfie. 'Here, Jack, take Sammy for a moment.' He gently lowered Sammy into Jack's arms and began to empty his inner pocket.

'Eleven, twelve.' He counted out the pennies. 'There you are, Sarah, one shilling. You go up to the Strand and see if you can get hold of a cab. Tell a story – someone tipped your poor little blind brother into the river . . .'

'And what about Mutsy?' enquired Tom.

'Tell him that your hero of a dog pulled the poor little boy out. Jack, you keep Mutsy back until the last minute. Don't want the cab driver changing his mind. Just slip him in with no fuss. Sarah, you keep the cab driver chatting while they're doing that.'

Sarah nodded and was gone.

'What'll we do if he won't take Mutsy?' Tom seemed unnerved by the silence after Sarah left. His voice was shaking.

'You keep rubbing Sammy's hands,' ordered Alfie. Tom would be better if he had something to do. He himself set to work on Sammy's ice-cold feet and Jack did the same. Mutsy had fallen again; Alfie could hear him panting and that added to his worries.

It seemed a long time before Jack said, 'Here she comes,' and then Sarah was beside them.

'He says he'll do it. He's getting out a tarpaulin for Sammy so that the wet doesn't damage his cab. Come on quickly, before he changes his mind.'

The cab driver was a tall, thin man with a head like a turnip. Like most cab drivers, out in all weathers every day, he wore a long overcoat with an extra cape over his shoulders. His hat had once been an expensive top hat, but the rain and fog had turned it silver-green and it had been bashed on its crown. Its brim framed his small round face like a halo. He was looking as if he wished he had driven away, but his face changed when he bent over Sammy and saw the angelic crop of blond curls, the sightless, milky eyes and the red line on his throat.

'Come on then, let's be having you.' He lifted Sammy out of Alfie's arms and placed him gently on top of the tarpaulin. Then he took his own rug and tucked it around the boy.

'The missus can give it a wash,' he said with a

wink at Sarah. 'So you've four brothers then, have you? Bet your mother and father have to work hard feeding the five of you.'

'That's right,' said Sarah, climbing up beside him on the outside seat. 'They work as cobblers, though, and they keep us busy. You'd be surprised the amount of work that goes into a pair of shoes. You'd never guess . . .'

She chatted on while Alfie and Jack hoisted poor old Mutsy into the cab. The dog was happy to lie down in the straw on the floor beside Sammy, and Alfie put a bit of the rug over him as well. The less that was seen of Mutsy, the better.

By now there were very few people left on the Strand. Even the cab drivers seemed to have given up for the evening and gone home to their own firesides. It felt quite eerie, driving along there through the yellow swirling fog.

The cab driver was an expert, though, and his horse was sure-footed and cautious. They went along slowly and carefully until they came to Wellington Street. They all breathed a sigh of relief when the cab safely made the turning and started the climb up towards Bow Street.

Although the streets were nearly empty, the newspaper boys were still crying the headlines to tempt people to buy the evening papers. It gradually dawned on Alfie that the same words were being shouted by all. He stuck his head out of the window of the cab and listened intently.

Yes, he had heard correctly.

'Girl arrested in Monmouth Street strangler case!'

So Betty was in the nick while the murderer roamed free.

CHAPTER 21

THE STRANGLER STRIKES AGAIN

Alfie did not hesitate. Instantly, he thrust his fist through the open window and knocked heavily on the cab roof.

'Stop at the police station!' he yelled.

'Shouldn't we get Sammy and Mutsy home?' Jack sounded hesitant. He seldom questioned Alfie's decisions.

Alfie did not reply. Jack was right, of course, but

he had a terrible fear that dry clothes and a hot drink weren't going to be enough. Every time a streetlight flickered into the cab, lighting up Sammy's white face and bloodless lips, he was filled with a terrible fear that his brother might be dying. He needed to get a doctor, and he could only think of one man who would be able to get a doctor for a crowd of ragged street urchins with only a few pence to their name.

'Wait here,' he said briefly and the instant the cab stopped, he was out, leaping lightly down from the high step and crossing the pavement to the Bow Street Station.

'Inspector Denham,' he said curtly to the constable behind the desk, and before anyone could stop him, he gave a knock on the inspector's door, pushed it open and then slammed it shut behind him.

The door was immediately re-opened by the constable, spluttering apologies to the inspector and threats to Alfie. The inspector himself jumped to his feet with an annoyed exclamation, but Alfie silenced both of them.

'The Monmouth Street strangler has struck again,' he said dramatically.

'What!' The two men hit the word at exactly the same second.

'Come with me,' said Alfie. He tried to sound assured and in charge. He had to get help for Sammy immediately. He elbowed the constable out of the way and opened the door for Inspector Denham as politely as he could.

They were both on his heels without another word. As he crossed the pavement, he didn't bother to glance around as the heavy tread of the constable kept pace with the quick light footsteps of the inspector. The newspaper boys' cries were muffled in the heavy fog, but Alfie wondered whether Betty could hear them from her cell.

'Afternoon, Inspector, Constable.' The cab driver had spotted the two and was off his box in a second, followed by Sarah. He threw open the cab door, holding the lantern high so that the light fell on the wrapped figure, lying very still on the seat.

Quick-witted Sarah folded back the rug, then slipped back out of the cab so that the inspector had a better view.

Sammy was as white as the marble statue of an

angel in nearby St Martin's church. His eyes were closed and the bright red mark of the strangler's wire appeared even redder on his pale throat. For a moment, even Alfie thought he might be dead, but Mutsy opened one eye, sniffed Sammy's hand and closed his eye again. Alfie's heart slowed down. His brother was still alive.

'Oh, dear God,' muttered the inspector. Then he whipped around towards Alfie. 'Who is this?'

'My brother.' Alfie watched the inspector carefully. Obviously the man thought Sammy was dead.

'Who did it?

'The Monmouth Street strangler.' The cabman, like all of his brotherhood, was quick off the mark. 'Look at the little fellow's neck.'

'But . . . but when?' The inspector sounded like a man who realises that he had made a mistake.

'Hour or so ago.' Alfie watched the inspector carefully as he bent over Sammy. There was a tiny twitch in his brother's eyelids. It was important that Sammy should be able to talk to the inspector. Alfie clenched his hands. There must be some way that he could restore Sammy to consciousness. Everything had to be done right, and it was up to him to do it. For a few seconds a wish crossed his mind that some adult could take charge, but he had long learned that such thoughts were dangerous and weakening, so he leaned over his brother and breathed into his ear.

'Now I lay me down to sleep,
My soul I give to God to keep.
And if I die before I wake,
I pray to God my soul to take.'

It had been his grandfather's prayer, always said before he tucked his grandsons into bed at night. Sammy especially had been very close to his grandad.

And it worked. The sightless eyes opened. His hand stretched out, touched Alfie's and then closed again.

'Who did this to you, Sammy?' asked Alfie urgently. 'Tell the inspector. Who tried to garrotte you?'

'A man.' Inspector Denham had to lean right into the cab as Sammy's weak voice whispered the words.

'Where did he find you?' Alfie was conscious that Inspector Denham had prodded the constable into opening his notebook. Now every word that Sammy uttered would be recorded.

'Monmouth Street . . . He was on a horse . . . He hit Mutsy . . .'

Rapidly and without saying a word, Alfie drew Inspector Denham's attention to the large wound on the poor dog's head. Mutsy, realising everyone was looking at him, rolled over and groaned and then waved all four paws in the air. Alfie tried to turn the sob which unaccountably passed his lips into a chuckle. He saw Sarah look at him, but avoided her gaze. Mutsy was feeling better. He was playing to his audience. Somehow the courage and spirit of the faithful dog was almost too much for Alfie.

'On a horse? Are you sure, sonny?' Inspector Denham bent over Sammy again.

'He pulled me up by the hair.' Sammy's voice was getting fainter. He would not be able to talk for much longer. His voice was getting weaker and the white eyelids dropped back down over his milky-blue eyes. The cabman put another rug over him and cleared his throat noisily. Tom wept quietly, his tears making pale trails down his grubby cheeks. Jack put an arm around his brother's shoulders. Alfie turned to Sarah.

'Tell the inspector what time Sammy left the

Montgomery house, Sarah,' he said urgently. He was fired with a passionate desire that the man who did this to Sammy should suffer for it. The inspector had to find him and arrest him. 'Sarah works as a scullery maid there,' he added.

'Just about two hours ago, or less,' said Sarah decisively.

'And it was a man who pulled Sammy on to the horse and hit the dog over the head,' said Alfie. He watched the inspector as carefully as he could as he repeated Sammy's words, '*It was a man and he was on a horse.* He's half-killed Sammy. I don't know if he'll recover. I wish I had the money for a doctor.'

'I see.' The inspector straightened up. Alfie could see him exchanging a look with the constable. When he spoke again, however, it was to the cabman.

'You're a charitable man to bring these children and their dog here,' he said. 'Could you drive them home and then do one more thing? Go to this address . . .' the inspector scribbled on a sheet torn hastily from the constable's notebook, 'and ask Doctor Goodsby to come and see this lad. Tell him I'll see that he is paid. Drive him to where the children live. Here's a half-crown for you.'

There was a chink of money in the inspector's waistcoat pocket and then the silver coin glinted in the lantern's light.

'Here's something to get an evening meal for the lot of you.' Again there was a fishing trawl in the deep pocket and another shilling was produced. Tom wiped the tears from his eyes with his sleeve and began to look more cheerful. Alfie took the money. There was something else that he had to say, though.

'What about Betts?' he asked, quickly pocketing the money.

'Who's Betts?' enquired the inspector.

Alfie ignored that.

'She wasn't the one that tried to kill Sammy.' He made his voice sound quite definite. 'Besides, a man in a top hat tried to murder me about an hour after Sammy was nearly done for.'

'Tried to murder you! You, too!' The inspector's glance sharpened. There was a moment's silence. The lantern flickered. A gas lamp popped. The newspaper boys continued to cry their news about the Monmouth Street strangler and Sammy closed his eyes again. Mutsy groaned, turned over on his front, tried to get up, but then collapsed again. Alfie swallowed hard.

'Let's go,' he said roughly. 'Can't hang around all night.'

'Yes, let's get that boy indoors.' The cab driver wanted to move on as well. 'Don't worry, Inspector, I'll fetch Doctor Goodsby and bring him around.'

Sarah had gone. Alfie discovered her absence when they started to get into the cab again. He did not comment and kicked Tom on the ankle when he started to say 'Where's —' She had nipped back to the cellar to get Mallesh out of the way, he guessed, trying to tell himself not to worry.

But he knew that he would not have another easy moment until the Monmouth Street strangler was caught and put behind bars.

CHAPTER 22

THE DOCTOR ARRIVES

When they got there, nobody but Sarah was to be seen, though Sammy's armchair had been pulled over to screen a dark corner and an old blanket had been thrown over it. Sarah had made a bed on the floor by the fire, and a large blackened kettle was simmering beside it. She had left the door to the cellar stairs open and a candle lantern on the bottom step. The cab driver carried Sammy down and laid him gently on the old cushions by the fire.

'Here you are, take this shilling back. The inspector has paid me,' he said before he left to fetch the doctor, handing over the twelve pennies to Sarah.

She took them hesitantly and he smiled, a wide crease in his turnip-like face, and settled his broken hat more firmly on his head.

'I don't suppose there is any ma and da,' he said, with a quick look around the bare cellar – the few boxes, the moth-eaten, threadbare cushions, the one broken chair and the few pewter jugs, 'just you and your brothers. Poor youngsters.' He hesitated for a moment and then added another shilling. 'Poor little fellow,' he said with feeling and with a last glance at Sammy. 'Who would do a thing like that to him? There are some very evil people in this world of ours.'

'And some very good ones,' said Sarah, accepting the money, her small teeth gleaming in a smile. She reached up and kissed the cabman's leathery cheek, and he grinned and patted her shoulder.

Alfie passed a shilling to Jack after the cabman had left. 'Keep that. You can buy sausages and beer after the doctor has been,' he said. If Sammy is taken to hospital, I'm going too, he thought. I'm never going to give the strangler a chance to get him again.

'Get a dry shirt, Tom,' he said aloud.

'I'll pour some water into this bucket,' Mallesh came out from behind the screening blanket.

'Here's a towel,' said Jack. 'Here, Tom, take those rags and rub down Mutsy, and Alfie and me will get Sammy out of those wet clothes. Should you be getting back, Sarah?'

'He looks terrible,' said Sarah, ignoring the question and bending over Sammy. 'Go on, quickly; get his clothes off. Haven't you got a better towel than this one? It's damp and dirty and full of holes. And it smells.'

'Take my turban,' said Mallesh, unwinding the folds of the six-foot piece of cloth to reveal jet-black hair, and holding it in front of the fire to warm it. 'It's clean,' he added to Sarah. 'I wash it each night.'

'Every night!' exclaimed Tom, bringing over an old yellowed shirt which had once belonged to Alfie's father.

'Wish that doctor would come,' muttered Alfie as

he rubbed his brother's cold body with the soft folds of Mallesh's turban.

'Funny he isn't a bit better,' agreed Jack in low tones as he pulled the dry shirt over his cousin's head. He, too, looked at Sammy's white face with concern.

'The cab's pulling up outside the pavement,' warned Tom as he peered up through the small narrow window in the wall of the cellar.

In a flash, Mallesh disappeared into his hiding place and Sarah took the lantern over to the door. A minute later Alfie heard footsteps stumbling on the steep stairs to the cellar.

Doctor Goodsby was a small, fat man carrying a large leather bag in one hand. He looked in a bad temper and Sarah wished that the cabman had come back down, too. The doctor had probably sent him on his way – too mean to pay for waiting time, she supposed.

'What's this, what's this?' asked the doctor fussily. He sniffed disdainfully and cast a contemptuous look around the untidy cellar.

'My brother was garrotted and flung in the river,' said Alfie stiffly.

The doctor bent over Sammy, carelessly pulling up one eyelid, and then he jumped back. Alfie watched him in silence. The doctor had a puzzled expression on his face.

'This is where the wire was tightened,' said Sarah, pointing to the throat.

'I'm not blind, girl,' he grunted. Once again, he pulled up Sammy's eyelid, frowned and then immediately delved into his leather bag, pulling out a tiny looking glass and placing it over Sammy's mouth. Alfie fought the desire to vomit, clenching his hands and taking small, shallow breaths through his nose. It seemed years before the doctor lifted the silver-backed glass and held it up. Alfie moved to stand beside him and forced himself to look.

The glass was damp. Sammy was still alive. Alfie dropped to his knees beside his brother, weak with relief.

'I'll have to bleed him,' said the doctor decisively. 'Here, you girl, hold this basin.'

From his bag he produced a white earthenware bowl with a half-circle cut out of it. Next came a pair of large scissors and a small, sharp knife. Quickly he cut one sleeve from the old shirt. Then he seized Sammy's arm. It fitted perfectly into the missing half-circle on the rim of the bowl. Sarah made a half-strangled sound as the doctor sliced into the boy's white arm. Immediately the blood dripped into the bowl. Every one watched silently until the bowl filled. The blood looked very red, thought Alfie, compared with Sammy's white face.

'Here's some laudanum. Give him some if he wakes.' The doctor seized his bag and marched quickly towards the door, saying briskly, 'Nothing to pay. Inspector Denham will see to that.'

'Wait.' Alfie went after him and caught the man by the sleeve. 'Will he be all right?'

The doctor shook him off and wrenched open the door. 'Maybe,' he said indifferently as he clumped up the uneven stairs. 'Don't like the look of those eyes, though.'

'He didn't know that Sammy is blind!' Sarah gasped as Alfie closed the door.

'And he's a doctor,' said Alfie with scorn. Tom gave a nervous giggle and then gulped.

'He should not do that. Take blood from the boy.

He needs his blood to make him strong again,' said Mallesh indignantly, coming out from his hiding place. 'We do not do this in India.' He came over and sat down beside Sammy, feeling his hands and rubbing them gently. He picked up the packet of laudanum and sniffed it. 'Opium,' he said and put it down again. 'Do not him give this until we can warm him.'

'You're right. He's still as cold as a stone,' said Alfie, taking Sammy's other hand.

'I'll fill some jars with hot water,' said Sarah, sorting through the pile of jars that Jack collected from houses in Bloomsbury. He got a halfpenny from the pickles factory for every ten jars.

'In India, the *hakim*, our doctor, would rub him like this,' said Mallesh. He set his long slim hands on Sammy's back and slowly began to massage him. 'I wished once to become a *hakim*. I had begun to learn, but then my father was hanged,' he remarked after a few minutes.

'Wrap the jars, Tom,' directed Sarah. 'Any old rags will do. Put them beside Sammy.'

Mallesh seemed tireless. His hands worked to a sort of rhythm, thought Alfie, almost like a man playing a drum, stroking, patting and tapping. And then he began kneading the flesh, like a baker getting the dough ready for the oven. Sammy's deathly white body seemed to be getting a glow. Sarah kept filling more bottles with hot water, Jack fed the fire, recklessly adding new coal as soon as the flames died down, Alfie paced up and down and Tom sat hunched up in the corner, biting his nails.

And then quite suddenly Mutsy stretched, groaned and got to his feet. Alfie poured some water into a tin bowl, but the dog ignored it. Walking slowly and unsteadily he came across to Sammy and started to lick his feet, almost seeming to copy Mallesh's massaging movements.

And then the miracle happened. Sammy opened his eyes, stretched out his hand. Alfie gripped it and Sammy said in a weak voice, 'God, Alfie, I'm hungry.'

CHAPTER 23

LIKE RATS FLEEING

Sammy fell asleep after eating two sausages and drinking some laudanum. He lay on the cushions in front of the fire, covered with blankets and with a couple of hot bottles on each side of him and one at his feet. His face was slightly flushed. From time to time, Alfie checked his hands and they felt warm.

'You saved my brother's life,' he said to Mallesh. 'I won't forget that.'

'I am not happy. I would like to get my herbs,' said Mallesh. 'When I left home, my mother gave me a box full of different herbs. It is with my things at the East India Docks. That river, your great river, that is not good to drink.'

'I think he will be all right. He did vomit up that water,' said Sarah. She got to her feet. 'I'll have to go now. The housekeeper is getting suspicious about this aunt that I keep visiting after going to the Ragged School. She asked me to bring my aunt to see her and I had to make up a story about her having a bad leg and not being able to walk. I think they'd all have a fit if they knew I was visiting a gang of boys in a cellar.'

Alfie didn't reply. There was too much to arrange. His mind seemed to be exploding with it. 'I was thinking that you shouldn't say anything at the Montgomerys' about Sammy being rescued,' he said after a minute.

Sarah nodded. 'I was thinking that myself. If the murderer is in the house, then let him keep thinking that he is safe.'

'Which one of them do you think it was, Sarah?' Alfie asked. 'Not the missus, or her man friend – he hasn't made an appearance for the last few months as far as you know, so how would he know about Sammy, or about me asking questions? That brings it down to the three men – the butler, Mr Denis or the visitor, Mr Scott. The butler would have known that Sammy was at the house and he saw me at the gate-keeper's lodge. The fellow that tried to hit me over the head wore a top hat. But the butler was wearing one of those when I saw him and the two toffs are bound to wear them, so that doesn't narrow it down at all.'

'The butler wouldn't go on horseback,' Sarah said. 'Well, I've never seen him, anyway.'

Alfie thought about that. It probably wasn't the but-ler, then, unless, of course, the coachman had asked him to exercise a horse. There didn't seem any reason why the visitor, Mr Scott, would have murdered Mr Montgomery. More likely to be the spoilt brat son. Alfie's mind was filled with an exploding hatred of Denis Montgomery. There he was, probably had every-thing handed on a silver spoon to him since he was half Sammy's age and then, just because his dad had come back from India and tried to put a stop to his gambling, he had murdered him and almost murdered poor old Sammy and faithful Mutsy, too!

Sarah took the lid off the pot of boiling water, peered into it and then added a few more pieces of coal to the fire. Jack cleaned out the frying pan with a rag and then sat quietly beside Alfie. Tom looked from one to the other, but said nothing either. He still looked subdued.

And then into the silence came a hoarse croak from Sammy.

'The one that smelled funny, he's the one that done it. The fellow that strangled me smelled funny.' His voice faded, and his eyes closed again. He seemed, thought Alfie, looking at him fearfully, like one who was halfway between life and death. Perhaps he shouldn't have given him that laudanum. Opium was bad for people. He had seen enough beggars die from it.

'I must go,' Sarah repeated.

'I'll come over tomorrow morning,' said Alfie. He picked up the lantern and went towards the door with her.

'Will that be safe?' asked Sarah.

'Safe enough . . . I know what to do and to say.' Alfie kept his voice sounding stout and confident, but even he could hear the false note of bravado. After one day there, Sammy had nearly been killed. Did he really want to venture into that place? On the other hand, if he didn't, he might never find out who the murderer was. Perhaps he and his gang would have to go into hiding, would have to live like rats fleeing from one cellar to another.

'I'll walk with you.' Mallesh was beside Sarah, sounding resolute. 'No one will see me in the fog. I want to get the herbs for Sammy. I'm not happy about him. He has a slight fever. And I'll get something for the dog's wound, also.'

And then they were both gone. Jack and Tom stretched out on the remaining cushions and Alfie sat beside his heavily sleeping brother. Through the window he could see the yellow haze of the gas lamp outside.

Perhaps it was the fog, but the air of London seemed to him to be thick with evil.

CHAPTER 24

ALFIE RISKS ALL

'Mallesh didn't come home last night.' Alfie's voice was sharp with anxiety as he faced Sarah in the small dark back scullery behind the kitchen of number one, Bedford Square.

He half-hoped that Mallesh had told Sarah something – perhaps that he had decided to stay the night in the lodging house at the East India Dock.

But Sarah's appalled face destroyed that last hope.

'He was going straight back to you as soon as he got the herbs,' she whispered, putting down the pan she'd been scrubbing. 'He said that it was important to get them into Sammy as soon as possible.'

'Any sign of a policeman?'

Sarah shook her head. 'No, there was no one really on the streets – except around St Giles – the usual drunken crowd there.'

'Did anyone in the house see him?'

'No, he just left me there by the stables.'

'He should never have gone near the house,' said Alfie. He could picture a shadowy figure watching from behind those tall, lace-draped windows.

Sarah wrung her hands. 'It's my fault, I shouldn't have let him come with me, but it was so creepy in the fog and besides he was telling me all about India – about the food that they eat and everything and we were here before I realised. I was such a fool.'

'I should have gone with you,' said Alfie, shaking his head.

'You had to stay with Sammy.' Sarah resumed her scrubbing of pans, efficiently rubbing them with coarse sand and then swilling them in a bucket. 'How is he?' she asked, slipping her feet into a pair of iron-soled pattens and clattering out into the yard to throw out the bucket of dirty water.

'He's better this morning. I gave him some more of the doctor's laudanum.' Alfie tried to sound relaxed, but his mind was churning through the possible reasons for Mallesh's disappearance. 'I'd better go up and tell the missus the sad news about my missing brother,' he said after a moment, with an attempt at a grin as Sarah wiped the tears from her eyes and pulled off her rough apron.

'Don't risk it,' she said nervously. 'You know what happened – what nearly happened – to Sammy.'

'I can look after myself.' Alfie knew that there was no point in backing out at this stage. He needed that money the inspector had half-promised him, but there was another more urgent reason. If the murderer were not caught, he and Sammy were in grave danger. He couldn't spend the rest of the winter looking over his shoulder, guarding Sammy, worrying all of the time.

'Leave it to the police,' said Sarah, reading his thoughts as usual.

'The police!' snorted Alfie. He had a poor opinion of the police so far. Hunting down an innocent Indian boy, dragging into prison a poor, sweet-natured girl like Betty. 'Come on, Sarah, let's go,' he said impatiently, seeing her shoulders shake.

Sarah was crying openly when they came into the kitchen, and the parlour maid and cook turned to stare at her and then at Alfie.

'The little blind boy never came home last night,' sobbed Sarah, and Alfie felt his own eyes sting. It was so nearly the truth.

'What!' The cook's eyes filled with tears and even Nora looked appalled.

'What'll the missus say?' Nora whispered.

'I'd better tell her,' said Alfie, trying to achieve a look that combined bravery with deep sorrow.

'I'll take him up,' said Nora. 'They're all in the breakfast parlour.'

Good – I might see them all, thought Alfie, as he followed Nora up the stairs. His bare feet felt the luxury of the thick carpet. Imagine having something like that on your floor! You would hardly need a bed.

Alfie followed Nora into the breakfast parlour.

'Excuse me, ma'am, sirs.' The parlour maid curtsied.

Alfie's mouth watered at the delicious smells coming from the silver dishes on the table. Mrs Montgomery and two men were there, all eating.

So which man owned the shadow on the lane, wondered Alfie, looking at the two men carefully. They were both big men, though not as tall as the butler. That must be Denis with the newspaper – he was much younger than the other man, and thinner too – though in a big winter coat the difference would be little in the outline of a shadow. Mr Scott had a bushy moustache and barely looked up from his breakfast. Could either of those two ordinary-looking gentlemen be the Monmouth Street strangler?

'Something terrible has happened, ma'am!' Nora was keen to be the first with the news. She gulped a little and then announced dramatically, 'That poor little blind boy didn't get home last night. Feared run over in the fog.'

'What!' Mrs Montgomery was on her feet with her two hands held high in the air to show how shocked she was.

'That's right, ma'am, and this is his brother come to tell the terrible news.'

Mrs Montgomery turned to Alfie. 'Oh, you poor boy,' she said emotionally. 'What a dreadful thing! Nora, one of the footmen must go straight to Bow Street Police Station and tell Inspector Denham that I want him to get a couple of men to search for this child. He may be lying hurt somewhere.'

'Inspector Denham knows all about it, ma'am,' said Alfie quickly. 'I'm just going up to Barts Hospital now. Inspector Denham thought my brother might have been taken there, but I wanted to come to see you first.' He gulped – it was surprisingly easy to do – and then waited a couple of seconds, lowered his voice and said in broken tones. 'It's . . . it's what . . . it's what Sammy would have . . . have wanted. You were very kind to him, ma'am.'

And that, he thought with satisfaction, should be worth a couple of pence at least.

'What about the dog?' asked Denis Montgomery suddenly. 'The dog went home with him, didn't it?' He lowered his newspaper and stared at Alfie, though his jaws still continued to munch the crisp slice of bacon. Alfie's heart began to beat a little faster. Was he looking into the eyes of a pitiless murderer – a man who would not even baulk at strangling a blind child and dropping his body into the river? This was a typical London toff's voice. What did the other one sound like?

'He's gone, too,' said Alfie with a quiver in his voice. 'He was a very good dog to my brother – always looked after him.'

'Poor children – you were alone in the world, were you?' Mrs Montgomery's eyes were glistening. 'Just the two of you?'

Alfie nodded. Her hand was going for her purse. She opened it and took out something. It was silver – he saw it gleam in the bright light from the gas lamp over the table.

'Give the boy this, Nora, and if he wants something to eat make sure that he has it.' She handed the coin to Nora, who took it with a sidelong glance at Alfie.

'Thank you, ma'am,' said Alfie. 'I'll be sure to tell you the news if I find my brother at the hospital.' He did his best to sound brave, or at least to sound as if he were trying to sound brave, but his eye was on the two men eating their breakfast. He wished that Mr Scott would speak, but he just went on munching his toast.

'Who was the man who asked about the dog?' Alfie whispered as he and Nora went down the stairs together. He knew it was Mr Denis, of course, but he hoped she might volunteer some new information about her employer's son.

'That was Mr Denis Montgomery. He's fond of dogs – fond of betting on them anyway,' said Nora. She didn't repeat the invitation to have something to eat and Alfie didn't bring up the subject. Nora gave Alfie the coin reluctantly, dropping it into the centre of his outstretched palm as if she feared to touch him. She would have liked to keep the coin, thought Alfie; it was a whole shilling! However, he thanked her for it as profusely as if she were the lady of the house herself, and Nora gave a stately nod.

There was a pudding-shop at the back of St Martin's church where you could get a pudding for a couple of pence. Alfie's mouth watered at the thought of it as he walked out of the back door, rubbing the shilling between his fingers. If only he could find Mallesh now, they would all have a great supper tonight with the money that was flowing in. He looked into the mews, but neither coachman nor groom was there so he made his way towards the gate.

'How's the betting slate getting on?' he asked, putting his head into the cosy lodge of the gatekeeper.

'Well, I've made one great bet with myself. There was an Indian came here last night – fellow in a turban, you know – and he was with the little scullery maid at number one. He hung around for a while – just to make sure that she got in safely I suppose – and guess what happened?' He waited expectantly, but Alfie just shook his head.

'Can't guess,' he said.

'Well, just as he was going to walk away from my gate, there was a big hullaboo and a lot of shouting and out rushed the butler with the groom and the coachman from number one and they grabs this fellow and they drags him off. They were going to take him down to the police station. I heard that all three of them have gone down to Bow Street this morning to swear evidence against him. '

'And what's the bet you made?' asked Alfie, trying hard to make his voice sound careless and uninterested.

'Have a look here, see what I wrote; see the bet that I made with myself about when this Indian will come back.'

Alfie looked at the slate. It didn't make any sense to him – it was just a whole lot of lines and curves – so he looked at the gatekeeper with as intelligent an expression as he could manage.

'That's right!' said the gatekeeper. 'I've put the word in great big capital letters. Look at it here: *NEVER.*' He gave a nod of satisfaction and added, 'Mark my words, we'll never see that Indian boy again.'

CHAPTER 25

SARAH IN TROUBLE

By the time Alfie reached Seven Dials, he realised that the footsteps he had heard behind him from time to time were still following him. They clopped along loudly, iron striking against the paving stones in a hurried, uneven fashion. He stopped and drew into the doorway of the Crown Inn and waited. He was not frightened, just curious. Today was not like yesterday. The day was misty, but the thick fog had gone and the streets were now full of people and, of course, he was not a blind ten-year-old, but a sharp-eyed twelve-year-old.

Still, it did sound a little like a horse, walking slowly, just as Sammy had described it. The clop-clop sound was getting nearer, and then it seemed to falter a little, just as if whoever followed him had become confused, had slowed to see whether their prey had escaped down an alleyway. Alfie peeped out cautiously and then gave a sigh of relief, mixed with exasperation.

'Sarah!' he called and then, as she straightened up and came nearer, 'What do you think you're doing?'

Now Alfie could see Sarah's face, and it was blotched and streaked with tears. She wasn't wearing her trim scullery maid's uniform either. She was dressed in some ragged clothes that looked as if they were far too small for her – a torn dress that barely reached to her knees and a ragged shawl, meant for a small child, tied around her shoulders, looking not much bigger than a handkerchief on a girl of her age. On her feet, instead of shoes, she wore a pair of pattens, her bare feet thrust into them and just about managing to hold them on as she staggered along on their raised platform.

'What . . .?' began Alfie.

'They've turned me off, sacked me,' said Sarah, trying to keep back her tears.

'Sacked you!'

'The butler had me up to his room just after you left. He accused me of being responsible for his master's death. Becky, the chambermaid, told him that Mallesh had seen me home. She was peeping out of the window when we came to the railings.'

'They saw Mallesh!'

Sarah nodded. 'That's right. The butler was going on about me being some sort of murderer myself. He and the housekeeper told me that I had to leave the house immediately. Cook wanted to keep me – she said that she had arranged that I would be getting everything ready for the meal tomorrow while the rest of the family and the servants and that Mr Scott were at the funeral. There would be no one left to keep the pots boiling because the missus said that she wanted every single one of the servants to attend the funeral – that didn't count me, of course. I don't count. Scullery maids never count.' Her eyes flashed angrily.

'The butler gave the orders – is he allowed to do that?'

'He's in charge of all the lower servants,' said Sarah. 'He and the housekeeper, together. The missus would have nothing to do with a small thing like a scullery maid being turned off without wages or even a character reference. I'll never get another job now.'

Alfie was thinking hard; ideas were beginning to form in his mind. But then he turned his attention back to Sarah.

'So they just threw you out on the street, just like that?' he said.

Sarah nodded and tried to smile. 'They kept all the clothes that I had been given and I had to wear these old things that I arrived in two years ago. And when I said that my old shoes didn't fit me any longer, the housekeeper said that I could take this pair of pattens.'

'What are you going to do?' asked Alfie.

'I don't know.' Sarah looked around. 'Perhaps some inn would have me to scrub floors, but it's the end of all my hopes for myself. I'd been thinking that if I worked hard as a scullery maid I might rise to being a parlour maid or even a cook. That's why I've been going to night classes in the Ragged School.'

'Well,' said Alfie, 'if we could just solve this case then you'd get taken back, wouldn't you?'

'That's right, I suppose.' Sarah tried to smile.

'Well, let's get working on it. Come back with me to the cellar and we'll talk to Sammy. He's a lad with brains. First we'll find you somewhere for tonight. I was thinking that Betts could probably find you a bed in her grandmother's place – just round the corner here.'

Sarah made a bit of a face, but she said nothing. The grandmother was an unpleasant old woman, but a night or two wouldn't hurt, thought Alfie, and guessed that Sarah was thinking the same thing. As they turned the corner, he was pleased to see Betty herself, walking towards them. She looked better than when he had last seen her.

'I got out,' she announced when she reached them.

'I know,' said Alfie. 'I was the one that got you out. I told the inspector that it couldn't be you because our Sammy was attacked and nearly strangled while you were sitting quietly in your cell.'

'Sammy!' Betty stared at him and then shivered.

Her face turned pale. 'Oh, poor little fellow! Is he all right?'

'He's fine, now,' said Alfie dismissively. 'Could you give Sarah a place to sleep in tonight, Betty? She's been dismissed because she was seen talking to an Indian. He's in prison now, but he didn't do that murder either.'

'So an Indian has been locked up – I suppose they have to find someone for the murder. Poor fellow, though!' Betty had a soft heart.

'I'm going to have to see Inspector Denham and sort out his ideas for him,' Alfie said grandly, 'but in the meantime is it all right for Sarah to doss down with you tonight?'

'Oh, yes,' said Betty. 'I'll make it all right with the old lady – tell her that you and Sarah got me out of the cells.'

'I'll be along later on then,' said Sarah. She sounded subdued. Alfie had never seen Sarah look so miserable. She was always quietly cheerful, always making the best of things.

'Why don't you take those pattens off your feet? You'd walk better. I don't know how anyone walks on things like that,' said Alfie, once Betty had gone down the steps and into her grandmother's cellar.

'I haven't gone in bare feet for two years,' said Sarah with a sigh. She bent down and slipped off the pattens. 'Do you think that we should have questioned Betty a bit more? After all, she was probably the last person to see Mr Montgomery alive.'

'No, I talked with her yesterday. She's got a brain full of air – nothing else in it. She had nothing useful to say.'

Suddenly Alfie stopped and stood there for a minute.

He was wrong, of course. Betty did have something to say. And she had already said it . . . And Sammy, his blind brother, had said the same thing and like a fool, he, Alfie, clever Alfie, had not noticed.

'Come on, Sarah,' he said. 'Let's get back quick. I want to ask Sammy something.'

CHAPTER 26

A STRANGE SMELL

'Where's Mutsy?' Alfie's voice was tense. He had warned Jack and Tom that they were not to leave Sammy alone, and they were there, the three of them in front of the fire, Sammy dozing in what was left of their grandfather's chair, but Mutsy was not in his usual position with his big head on Sammy's feet, guarding him until Alfie came home.

'He's dead.' There was something strange about

Tom's voice as he glanced towards a dark corner, but Alfie did not pause. He rushed over.

And there was Mutsy lying there, not moving . . .

Alfie said nothing. There was an enormous lump in his throat and to his horror he heard the sound of a great sob escape him. Tears were pouring down his face.

'Come alive, Mutsy!' At Tom's voice, the big dog instantly jumped to his feet and tucked his head under Alfie's arm. His tail was wagging so hard it raised a cloud of dust from the old trunk that held their few poor belongings, and his hot tongue licked the tears from Alfie's face as the boy bent over him.

'You was taken in!' Tom's voice held a jeering note.

'No, I wasn't, I knew you were just fooling,' Alfie retorted immediately, but his heart was still thumping in his chest.

'You're so stupid!' Sarah rounded on Tom, boxing his ears fiercely. 'And you, Jack! Why didn't you stop him? Why don't you do something useful with your time, the two of you? Come on, then, get this place cleaned up a bit. Alfie has important business with the police inspector and it may be that he will bring him back. Go on, get a wet rag; clean up that trunk. It's filthy. Jack, you get that bucket and wipe down that window. Be quick about it, the two of you.'

'It was just a joke,' said Tom sulkily, but Sarah was in no mood to listen to him.

'Go on – rub that properly. This place is a disgrace. Have you got a broom?'

Alfie joined Sammy by the fire. 'How are you doing?' he asked casually, seeing that the shouting had woken up his brother. He kept his hand on Mutsy's warm fur.

'I'm all right.' Sammy's voice shook and Alfie looked at him closely. The red line, the mark of the murderer's garrotting wire, had faded to a dark colour, but Sammy was very pale. It would take a while for him to get over this. Alfie wished that Mallesh were there to give another of his massages, or even try his herbs.

'Most of the dirt is on the outside of the window, Sarah,' said Tom plaintively.

'Well, get outside and clean it then,' said Sarah smartly.

'Oh, leave the cleaning for the moment,' Alfie said impatiently. 'What does it matter? This place is no

Buckingham Palace; everyone knows that.'

Tom and Jack laughed a lot at that joke and dropped the rags back into the bucket with relief. Sarah made a face, but said nothing.

'We need to put our heads together to solve this case of the Monmouth Street strangler,' said Alfie. He waited until they were all sitting around him, gathering his thoughts and shifting ideas to the front and back of his mind. It didn't hurt to keep them all waiting – he was the gang leader and everyone understood that.

'Mallesh has been banged up as the murderer,' he said, 'and Sarah here has lost her job because they think she's mixed up with him. So it's more important than ever to find the real strangler.' There was a shocked silence until he went on. 'First of all, we'll hear what Sammy has to report from the day that he spent at the Montgomery house. You're feeling well enough now, Sam, are you? You've slept off most of that laudanum stuff, have you?'

'Most,' said Sammy in a low voice. 'Gives you horrible dreams, though, that stuff.'

'Perhaps we should leave him alone for a while,'

suggested Jack, but Alfie shook his head.

'Do him good to talk about it. What was the most interesting bits of your day as a knife boy, Sam?'

It took Sammy a bit of an effort to bring that back. What had happened after he left Bedford Square was still at the front of his mind. After a minute, though, he had sorted out his thoughts.

'I suppose there were a few things,' he said slowly. 'The trouble is that I don't know which one was which.'

'Just tell it the way it happened,' advised Alfie.

'Well, I was put in the butler's parlour and then a man came in to have breakfast. And then another man came in and I heard him ask the first fellow if he had found Coutts bank and then I think the first one gave the second one money. I think this second fellow was probably the butler. And then he went out and another man came in – he started eating breakfast this time.'

'A third man,' said Jack thoughtfully.

'So the second man didn't eat anything?' asked Tom.

Sammy shook his head. 'I don't think so,' he said.

Alfie's heart sank. Sammy still sounded very

confused. Perhaps he would have to leave the questioning for another few hours.

'It does sound as though the second man was the butler,' said Sarah. 'But why was he getting money from Mr Denis, or Mr Scott for that matter?'

'Perhaps the butler was blackmailing the murderer,' said Alfie. 'About the time he came back home on the night of the murder, maybe, or the butler found the garrotting wire in his room, or something like that. That's the way that I see it. Go on, Sammy. Did they talk about anything – Mr Denis and Mr Scott – while they were eating their breakfast? Take your time, just tell us whatever comes into your head.'

'Nothing much,' said Sammy, 'but I'll tell you something, neither of them sounded normal. They were both uneasy-like – afraid, I'd say.'

'I see.' Alfie thought about that. He relied absolutely on Sammy's instincts. But why were *both* men afraid?

'One more thing,' said Sammy. 'When I was going away I heard one man ask the other if I had been in the butler's pantry all of the time – and I'll tell you something else – he sounded furious.'

'So it looks like either Mr Denis Montgomery or Mr Scott did it,' said Sarah.

'That's right,' said Alfie. 'But which is which?'

'Have we any more clues?' asked Tom. 'It's a pity that old Sammy couldn't see the man that took him up on the horse.'

'He could do something almost as good,' said Alfie – trust Tom to say something stupid like that! 'He could smell him. Tell us about that smell again, Sammy.'

'It was a funny sort of smell.' Sammy's voice shook, but he controlled it and went on trying to sound as if he didn't care. 'It wasn't soap, but it was a bit like soap, sort of sharp – not sweet.'

'Sour?' asked Sarah, but Sammy shook his head.

'Flowery?' asked Tom, but Sammy shook his head again.

'Perfume? Like you smell from the ladies coming out of the theatre?' Jack was used to spending a lot of time around Covent Garden, holding horses' heads, or helping carriage drivers who were assisting ladies out of the vehicles.

'There's something in this,' said Alfie. He looked all

around to make sure that everyone was listening. 'When I talked to Betty of Monmouth Street, she said that the man who was following herself and Mr Montgomery smelled funny. Not bad, not the soapy smell of your usual toff – Betty would know that – no, she just said that he smelled funny.'

'And?'

Alfie ignored that. Jack was a good fellow, very reliable and much more sensible than Tom, but he didn't have the brains of his cousins. Alfie turned his face towards Sammy.

'You said the same just now, didn't you, Sam? A funny sort of smell. What kind of smell? Try to think.'

'Not soap – you're right there, Alfie.' Suddenly Sammy sounded better. 'I don't think it was soap – more like something you smell from an apothecary's shop. I'd know the smell again. That's right – some-one in the drawing room smelled of it that time I was singing a hymn to your missus, Sarah.' Sammy's face was alert and interested. He looked more like himself again.

'Would you know, Sarah?' Jack was eager to join in

the discussion, but Alfie wasn't surprised when Sarah shook her head.

'I've never noticed,' she said apologetically. 'I didn't have anything to do with the family or the guests. I wasn't allowed upstairs. I was always in the scullery. I'd sleep in a little room off the scullery and never go anywhere else in the house, except to the butler's pantry, of course. He keeps the knives there.'

'Mallesh smelled of that same smell – just a little bit – on the first day when he came here,' said Sammy suddenly. 'I remember thinking to myself: *what's that smell?*'

'Just that first day?' Alfie's mind was working fast. He hugged Mutsy, feeling some of the excitement that Mutsy felt when he tracked down those huge rats near Smithfield Market. Quickly he got to his feet.

'I'm just popping around to have a little word with my friend the inspector,' he said. 'Jack, you take Mutsy for a little walk. Sarah, you go with him and see if the butcher will spare him a nice big bone. Tell the story about him rescuing Sammy from the river and getting a bash on the head. Make a good story out of it. Oh, and Tom,' Alfie's voice hardened, he hadn't forgiven

Tom for pretending that Mutsy was dead, 'you get this place cleaned up, or no supper for you – and I can tell you I'm planning on something pretty good.'

'You again!'

Alfie was definitely not the constable's favourite visitor to the Bow Street Police Station.

'Me again,' agreed Alfie. 'Might I have a word with the inspector?'

'He's out,' replied the constable triumphantly. 'Perhaps you'd like to tell me what your business here is.'

Alfie thought for a moment. He doubted he would be successful, but there was no harm in asking.

'I'd like to visit the Indian prisoner – as an act of Christian charity,' he added, remembering the preacher who once tried preaching the word of God to the busy crowd around Covent Garden. Sammy's hymn had proved more popular than the preacher's words, and they all had a good supper that night.

'Well, you can't visit the Indian prisoner.' The constable had a sneering note in his voice, but Alfie ignored that.

'Why not?' he asked briskly.

'Because he ain't here. Was released two hours ago. No manners, these young ruffians,' the constable added, talking to himself as if Alfie had already left the police station.

Why had Mallesh not come back to them, then? wondered Alfie as he crossed the road and made his way back to the cellar. Ahead of him he could see Jack and Sarah with Mutsy proudly carrying a huge bone with several pieces of meat still attached to it. That would keep him satisfied for another day – soon he would be back to hunting for himself again.

Alfie caught up with them but did not speak. His mind was too busy.

Mallesh was the problem, he thought as he went ahead of the others, slowly down the dark stairs. How on earth could he ever find Mallesh in the teeming streets of London?

And if he didn't find him, and get him to identify that smell, how would Alfie ever be able to solve the murder?

CHAPTER 27

A MOUTH LIKE THE DEVIL'S

The cellar was very dark when they opened the door – the fire was low, just casting a subdued glow and for a moment Alfie could see no one. Mutsy, however, had no doubt. Dropping his bone with a loud thud, he gave a quick, sharp bark, dashed forward, tail waving like a flag, and rushed up to the figure beside Sammy. Another bark and a wet lick and then he was back to pick up his precious bone and retire to a dark corner with it.

By now Alfie could see the figure. It was Mallesh, grinning widely.

'Mallesh and me have solved the problem for you,' said Sammy placidly. 'You'd better talk to him quick before he has to go. He's signed on for a passenger ship going to India tonight.'

Sarah gasped. 'How did you get out of the police station?'

'I told the inspector that it was not possible for me to murder Mr Montgomery,' said Mallesh. 'I told him my friend knows that I was there at the lodging house all that evening and night. The inspector sent his man over to the East India Docks to bring back my friend to question him.'

'Why didn't you say that before?' asked Jack.

'I had thought Mr Montgomery was murdered in the morning,' explained Mallesh. 'That's what I heard at the window when the inspector was talking to you.'

Alfie understood. The inspector had said that the body was found in the morning, and Mallesh must have assumed that the murder had just happened. However, there was something more important to be dealt with. 'What's that smell?' he asked, sniffing.

Mallesh opened his mouth and blew strongly in Alfie's direction. It did make the sharp smell much stronger – but that was not what filled Alfie's mind with a sudden surge of excitement.

The fire had flared up and Mallesh's widely opened mouth was clearly visible.

He had a mouth like the devil's, all bright red, tongue and all – that's how the gatekeeper had described the visitor to the Montgomery household.

'Mr Scott!' exclaimed Alfie.

'Oh, *shabash*!' exclaimed Mallesh. His very white teeth flashed in a grin of congratulations.

Sammy laughed. It was good to hear the sound. He was more himself today. An empty mug with some green leaves around the edges stood beside him. No doubt, Mallesh had given him a herbal drink.

'See, Mallesh? I told you that Alfie here was a fly bloke.'

'*Dekho*,' said Mallesh taking something out of his mouth and pointing to it. 'This is an Indian nut, wrapped in betel leaves. That's what the smell is. That makes the red colour.'

'Only someone who has been to India would have these betel leaves,' said Sammy excitedly. 'That's what Mallesh has been telling me. Chances are that Mr Montgomery's son wouldn't have got hold of them, or have the habit in the first place – but Mr Scott has just come back from India.'

'Why do people chew them?' asked Sarah curiously, sitting down on the rag rug in front of the fire.

'Makes you feel good – makes you . . . calm,' said Mallesh. 'I got some when I got the herbs for Sammy. My friend at the lodging house had my things safe.' Once again he opened his mouth to let them see the red dye and smell the queer sharp smell.

'But why should Mr Scott murder Mr Montgomery?' Sarah sounded puzzled.

'Perhaps they had a fight,' suggested Jack.

'Don't think that was it,' replied Alfie. 'From what Betty said, the murderer was shadowing the two of them, and when she left Mr Montgomery, he moved in with his garrotting wire. She smelled the . . . what are they? The betel leaves. She smelled them and that's what she told me – that he smelled funny. And of course, Sammy said the same thing. The man on the horse smelled funny, that's right, isn't it, Sam?'

'It doesn't make sense, though,' said Sarah. 'It would make much more sense if it was Mr Denis. He could murder his father, inherit all the wealth and pay off his gambling debts. Like we were talking about the other day.'

'She's right,' said Jack, and Alfie nodded. That did make sense, but he believed Mallesh when he said that only someone from India would have that habit.

'Perhaps you could talk to the inspector and get him to look for clues,' said Sarah, but her voice sounded dubious and Alfie knew that this would not be a good idea.

'Better for us to find out the reason first,' he said wisely. 'We've more brains than them fellows down at the police station.'

There was a silence. Alfie looked around. Tom was poking a stick into a gap in the fire and Jack was running his fingers through his dark hair. Sarah was turning her pattens over and over in her hands, Mallesh had his eyes closed and was chewing placidly on his betel leaves' mixture and Sammy's sightless eyes seemed to be fixed on the fire. Only

Alfie would have known that the blind boy was thinking hard.

Sammy was the one that broke the silence. 'What about the diamond belonging to Mallesh's father?' he asked.

Alfie gazed at him. There was no doubt that young Sammy had brains. Mallesh opened his eyes and smiled sleepily. 'I have decided to forget the diamond,' he said. 'The inspector was very kind to me. I think he believed my story, but he said that he cannot give the diamond back to me. But he gave me a letter for the police in my hometown to look into the matter. And, another thing – this is very good for me – he gave me a police certificate to take to the East India Docks to say I can work on passenger ships as an attendant. So now I have a new job. I will make much more money on those ships than I did on the trading ships and then I will study to be a *hakim*.'

'You'll make a very good one,' said Alfie warmly. 'You was the one that cured old Sammy here.'

'And your mother will be glad to see you come back,' said Sarah softly.

Mallesh nodded and then he looked curiously at

Sammy, whose face was still turned towards the fire. 'What are you thinking of, Sammy?' he asked.

'You see, if there was one diamond in the ground,' said Sammy turning around, 'then there might have been more. Alfie, do you remember how Grandad used to tell us stories of how in Ireland people saw gold in the streams, and then when they dug into the mountain they found so much gold that they had their hearts' desire.'

Alfie said nothing. He had always thought these tales of his grandfather had been fairy stories, but he was surprised to see Mallesh nodding vigorously.

'You're right, Sammy,' he said. 'I did not think of that. It is true. Where one diamond lies, fifty more may be hiding deep down in the earth and ready to be found.'

'Perhaps there is a diamond mine in the place where your father found the diamond, Mallesh.' Sammy sounded like someone going step by step through some well thought-out matter.

'Would that land have been owned by Mr Montgomery?' queried Sarah.

Mallesh nodded vigorously. 'Yes,' he said. 'But not

just by Mr Montgomery, remember they are . . . are together – a pair.'

'Partners,' said Sarah.

'Yes, partners.' Mallesh nodded again. 'Mr Montgomery and Mr Scott.'

'And now that Mr Montgomery is dead, then Mr Scott might be the owner,' suggested Jack.

'Surely he would have to share it with Mr Denis, though,' argued Sarah. 'That's the law. I heard that from the man that runs the Ragged School. He said that if a rich man dies, then his eldest son inherits all his land and property. The wife only gets whatever has been settled on her when she was married. Mr Denis will be able to afford his gambling now his father is dead.'

'Are we going back to having this Denis as the chief suspect, then?' asked Jack.

'It's a puzzle, isn't?' said Alfie. He understood how Jack felt. 'On the one hand, Mr Scott looks guilty because of Sammy and Betty smelling these betel leaves from the murderer – and the gatekeeper saw Mr Scott with a red mouth and red teeth, just like Mallesh has now.'

'But on the other hand,' said Jack slowly, 'it seems as if Denis has more to gain. Don't forget, we are only guessing about this diamond mine. We may be quite wrong.'

'You're right, Jack,' said Sarah quietly. 'We need some more evidence.'

Mallesh rose to his feet. 'You will have to think. I wish I could help, but I must go now. My ship sails tonight. I just came back to say goodbye to you all.'

'And one day, when you've made money and you are working as a *hakim* you might come back and show the English doctors how to cure sick people,' suggested Sammy, feeling the cut on his arm gingerly.

'And perhaps some day I might come out to India,' said Sarah softly. 'I'd like to see those snow-covered mountains that you were telling me about, and to sit in a sari in the hot sun and watch elephants go down the road.'

'Good luck with everything, Mallesh.' Jack's voice was warm as he clapped Mallesh on the shoulder.

'Good luck,' echoed Tom.

'I'll see you to the door,' said Alfie gruffly. When he got there he didn't quite know what to say, but eventually he squeezed Mallesh's hand. 'I'll never forget what you did for Sammy,' he said.

'And I'll never forget you all. You have been family to me,' said Mallesh solemnly. 'You believed me from the beginning and you protected me and fed me.'

He put the two palms of his hands together, said '*Namaste*' and bowed in farewell. Then he was gone, leaving behind the faint tang of the sharp, clean-smelling betel leaves.

'I have an idea, Alfie,' said Sarah. 'Tomorrow everyone will be out of the Montgomery house between eleven and twelve. They'll all be at the funeral. Why don't we go and have a look through Mr Scott's bedroom? We might find something.'

'How would we get in?' The idea appealed to Alfie, but he was annoyed that he hadn't thought of it himself.

'Through the mews and then in through the scullery door. The key is hidden in an old pot outside the scullery. Cook told me to leave one there when I got permission to go to the Ragged School as soon as my work was done each evening, so I could let myself in if I came back late. I bet no one has thought to take the key away.'

Sarah and Alfie looked at each other. A smile began to form on Alfie's lips. He liked the idea of this. Usually, if you took a chance, something turned up. This would be much better than trying to explain to the inspector that because a blind beggar boy and a poor girl from Monmouth Street had smelled betel leaves, the murderer had to be Mr Scott. He would never be believed. But who knew what they might find in the bedroom – even some betel leaves would help. This was just the sort of adventure that he liked.

'Tomorrow, then, at eleven,' said Alfie.

'Tomorrow at eleven,' repeated Sarah, as she rose to go to Betty's place for the night.

'Be careful,' said Sammy quietly, as he stroked Mutsy's head. 'That Mr Scott is a dangerous man.'

CHAPTER 28

ENEMY TERRITORY

The fog had seeped away overnight. Heavy black clouds replaced it, making narrow Monmouth Street as dark as if the day had decided to end almost as soon as it had begun. Small triangles of candle flames burned inside most windows and the lamplighter had already propped his ladder against a gas pole, his lighter in hand.

Sarah appeared so quickly that Alfie knew she had

been waiting for him. Neither spoke as they made their way to Bedford Square. Alfie guessed that she was nervous, but he couldn't think what to say. He kept throwing quick glances over his shoulder, expecting to see a giant, top-hatted shadow on the road behind them.

The mews at the back of the Bedford Square houses were busy. Almost every stable had men working on horses, brushing them, cleaning out the straw, putting in new straw, putting hay in the feeding racks, all except for the stables behind number one. These were silent and empty. All were at the funeral.

Sarah went confidently down the steps, through the yard and then slipped around the corner. Alfie followed her and Sarah already had the scullery door unlocked by the time he reached her. Luckily the yard had been swept clean so their bare feet did not leave marks on the luxurious carpet as the two of them raced up the main staircase, passing gold-framed mirrors, white marble statues and a marvellous stair window with pictures made from coloured glass. Alfie wished he could stop and study these, but he knew that he shouldn't. There had been no servants in the kitchen, but that did not mean that some of them would not be coming back after the church service, and before the burial, in order to get the lunch ready for the mourners.

'Where are the bedrooms?' asked Alfie, but Sarah shook her head, looking around her helplessly.

'I told you; I was never allowed upstairs,' she whispered.

'That's where the drawing room was; the bedrooms are probably up the next set of stairs.' Alfie had spent quite some time staring at the house from the gate-keeper's shelter and he remembered the three rows of windows. The upper servants would probably be in the attics, so the bedrooms would be in the top row.

'Not that one,' whispered Sarah as Alfie opened the first door when they reached the top of the stairs. 'That must be the missus's.' It did look like a woman's room, with pretty flowery hangings on the bed and a table piled high with little boxes and jars in front of a tall looking glass.

'Not this one either.' The second room obviously led from the woman's room and the doors were set open between the two rooms. This was probably Mr

Montgomery's room. The furniture was darker and the curtains plainer.

'I'd say this is Mr Denis Montgomery's room,' said Sarah after a pause while they gazed into the third room. 'There's such a lot of things here – a visitor wouldn't have this many bits and pieces, and look – that looks like a boy's cricket bat. Why would Mr Scott bring that all the way from India? They'll be back soon,' she added nervously. 'They won't be gone for long.' Her voice was trembling and she jumped when a loud explosion sounded.

Alfie jumped too. 'Sounds like a gun,' he said. He glanced out of the window and saw jagged streaks of lightning cross the sky. 'Just thunder,' he said with an attempt at a laugh. He didn't like thunder much, but he didn't want to admit it in front of Sarah. He turned his back on the sky, marched out of the room and followed her in through the next door.

'This looks like Mr Scott's room.' Alfie's voice was full of satisfaction as he gazed into the fourth room. It was bare and tidy, and a labelled trunk stood in the middle of the floor, with a few tightly packed leather bags arranged beside it. In fact, he thought, everything was so neat and orderly that it looked as though Mr Scott planned to leave the house soon after the funeral was over. He walked over towards the bags and then suddenly another clap of thunder ripped through the air. He jumped. 'What's that? Something moved there.'

'That's just the looking glass. You saw yourself in it.'

Alfie spun around. The room was filled with a strange light and opposite him he saw a boy in ragged clothes.

'My ghost, maybe.' Alfie tried to joke, but his voice was trembling. He looked all around the room, trying to imagine that he was a police inspector.

There was only one thing out of place in the room. In the corner, by the window, there was a tall sloping desk, just like the ones at the police station. On it there was an inkwell with a quill stuck into it, a piece of sealing wax flung down beside the flintlock tinderbox for melting it, and a tin canister with its lid lying next to it. A piece of white paper with marks on it lay beside it, pushed askew as if someone had carelessly dislodged it before leaving the bedroom.

'He was writing a letter,' said Sarah, moving over.

'I suppose he took it with him. What's that for?'

Alfie pointed at the white paper.

'Oh!' There was another clap of thunder. Sarah had been in a state of nerves ever since she had entered the house.

'Take no notice of it,' said Alfie firmly. 'What's written there?'

'That's blotting paper. They dry the ink with that. I can't read the word. It's backwards. Wait, though. Nora had a piece of blotting paper that she'd picked out of the waste-paper basket from Mrs Montgomery's bedroom. She's very nosy, Nora, and this is what she did to read it.' Quickly she went over to the looking glass and held it up.

'It's to a bank in the Strand,' she said after a minute. 'I'm not sure how to pronounce the first word. It's either *Cowts* or *Coots*. It's spelled C-o-u-t-t-s.'

'*Coots*, I think,' said Alfie firmly. 'Do you remember Sammy heard the butler ask the man at breakfast if he had found Coutts Bank? Now, did he take this letter with him, or could it be in his bag?'

In a second he had the smallest leather bag up on a chair and unsnapped the catches. There was another crash of thunder, but in his excitement he ignored it.

'There it is,' he said immediately, taking out a sealed and stamped envelope. 'Right on the top of his bag. Got its penny black stamp already on it, too. Go on, Sarah, read it.' With an effort he kept his voice steady. Sarah was nervous enough already. She would be worse if he, too, betrayed any nerves.

Sarah gasped as he recklessly broke the seal and tore open the envelope, but she took the sheet of paper in her trembling fingers.

Alfie waited. From the square he heard the noise of a heavy front door slam closed. He reckoned it was a few doors down, but even so he could not help giving a slight jump. Sarah was screwing up her eyes in an effort to make out the words on the page. She had learned to read at the Ragged School – she had often suggested that he should go, but he had never wanted to bother. It had all seemed too difficult.

But how well could she read?

'It's not easy,' she said after a moment.

'I'll just have another look through his bags and see if I can get any clue there. Perhaps I'll find some of those betel leaves and those nuts that Mallesh was telling us about.' Alfie felt that he could not bear to stand there, doing nothing, for another moment.

'No, wait. I'm getting the hang of it now. It's just that he makes some of the letters in a funny way. Listen.

'*Messrs Coutts & Company, The Strand, London.*

'*Dear Sirs, I enclose the deed to the diamond mines in Calcutta. I also enclose a report from an engineer in which you will see that the diamond mines, after years of being considered a failure, have started producing good quantities of fair-sized diamonds.*

'*Please note that I am now the sole owner of the mines according to the deed of agreement between myself and the late Mr Montgomery. I believe you have that deed in your possession.*

'*In view of the number of diamonds which are now being found on a daily basis, I'm sure that you will have no problem in giving me a draft for two thousand pounds which I will need for covering my expenses in developing the mines on my return to India.*

'*Please reply to my address in India, as I am leaving London this evening.*

'*Yours faithfully, R. Scott.*'

Alfie stared at Sarah. 'Sammy was right. So that's why he murdered Mr Montgomery. Now he can have the diamond mines to himself, instead of just half of them. Quick, give me the letter. This is better than any betel leaves. Let's go.'

'Hush,' said Sarah. 'Listen!'

There was the sound of the big mahogany front door downstairs being opened with a key and then slammed closed again. Heavy footsteps sounded in the hall. Heavy footsteps clumped up the stairs, getting nearer and nearer . . .

Alfie and Sarah looked at each other in horror. They were trapped!

CHAPTER 29

THE MAN WITH THE GUN

'Quick,' whispered Sarah. 'We'll hide in one of the cupboards.'

'No, he'll miss the letter, and then he'll come looking for us.'

'Well, leave the letter then!'

'Not on your life! Come on!' Alfie seized Sarah by the hand and dragged her through the French window leading on to the balcony. Carefully he inched the window shut after them and then looked around. Yes, he had remembered correctly.

Some tall tree-like creeper grew up the wall from the ground, stretching its way right up to the roof. Now, in November, it was blackened and dead, but the strong trunk and side branches still remained, and that should be easy enough to climb. Luckily they both had bare feet. Alfie made a quick decision. To go down would be fatal – if Mr Scott came to the window, he was bound to look down first of all and then shout to the gatekeeper to stop them. No, the only safe thing would be to go up and hide on the roof for a while.

'Go on,' Alfie said, giving Sarah a push towards it with one hand while with the other he rolled up the letter to Coutts Bank and shoved it deep into his pocket.

And then he almost lost his grip as another flash of lightning came, followed instantly by a terrible crash, and then a heavy silence.

Sarah was a good climber, quick and neat and he was on her heels immediately, listening all the time for sounds from within the house. Yes, Mr Scott had discovered the missing letter. Alfie could hear the exclamation when he clicked open the bag. He grinned to himself, picturing Mr Scott wondering whether he had put the letter in the bag after all. Then another faint click. The trunk was being opened.

Alfie was suddenly worried that he could hear all the sounds from the bedroom so clearly – perhaps the window wasn't quite shut. He daren't tell Sarah to hurry, as his own voice might carry to the man in the bedroom.

Now they were passing the small windows at the top of the house. These would be more bedrooms. If one had been left open it would have been tempting to go in and then creep down the back stairs, but they were firmly closed.

There was a violent crash as the French window was flung open and slammed against the wall, followed by the sound of a heavy footstep.

And then the rain began, long lines of it slanting down from the sky and soaking them through in less than a minute. Both of them stopped, clinging desperately to the thinner stems of the top of the creeper, trying not to be swept off by the terrible cloud burst.

Alfie risked a quick glance down. Mr Scott was on the balcony, but he was not looking up. He was looking down, leaning over the rail and scrutinising the pavement below.

Only two more minutes and they would be safe. Sarah was now quite near to the roof. He could see her hand reach up and clutch on to the white-tiled parapet which reared up like a tiny wall to hide the gutter pipe.

But just as Alfie had begun to take the final few steps to safety, one of the white tiles broke off and fell down to the iron railings of the balcony with a crash. Alfie heard a sudden curse. He looked down and straight into Mr Scott's eyes. For a moment, Alfie froze, but then Mr Scott dived back into the bedroom.

'Quick, Sarah, quick!' Alfie hissed. 'Get over the parapet, get up to the chimney. Get behind it! I'm just behind you.'

It was too late, though, for him to follow her. In two seconds, Mr Scott was back out on the balcony.

There was another explosion. No lightning, though. Nor thunder, either. Alfie risked another glance and saw a gleam of light from something round and metallic clutched in Mr Scott's big fist.

Mr Scott was pointing a small revolver straight at him. The explosion had been a shot.

'Murderer!' yelled Alfie. 'Murderer, murderer, murderer!' he continued to yell as he dropped over the parapet and sank to his knees. He had little hope of anyone hearing him, though, as the thunderstorm still continued. A shot whizzed past him, striking the edge of the parapet, then another shot and another. Four, five shots. Although he was soaked to the skin Alfie felt hot sweat flood his armpits. The terrible sour taste of vomit filled his mouth.

And then there was another flash of lightning and a crack of thunder. Or was it thunder? No, it must have been a bullet. A small piece of tile fell down past his eyes. Desperately he tried to flatten himself against the roof edge. Sarah had managed to wedge herself behind the chimney, but Alfie didn't dare to move or else he would risk a bullet in the spine.

But no new shot came. Alfie peeped down. There was no sign of Mr Scott on the balcony. Perhaps the revolver only held six shots. He had probably gone back into the bedroom to reload. Was there any way to escape? Alfie looked in despair at the tightly closed windows of the servants' bedrooms.

But then he suddenly realised that a window was open in the roof of the next-door house. The lightning began to flash again and the thunder crashed at almost the same moment, but Alfie welcomed it. No man would be able to fire accurately into that blazing sheet of light.

'Quick, Sarah!' he yelled. 'Get along the roof. Get in through the window!' He began to break off pieces of the damaged parapet tiles and stack them beside him rapidly.

The lightning continued to flash, but there were longer intervals between its flares and the crash of thunder. Soon the storm would die out. They had to escape within the next few minutes, he knew, as he watched Mr Scott come out on to the balcony again, pistol in hand.

But Sarah was in through the window. Now for his plan.

For a second, he revealed himself deliberately, hurling a piece of parapet tile to distract the man's aim. The shot went wide, hitting the wall, well over to the left of Alfie. Once again he rose up and hurled another piece of tile, and once again a shot rang out.

Two, thought Alfie, and then *three, four*. 'Come on, come on,' he said aloud, and then shot a lump of cement over to the left of him. It worked. Mr Scott sent two shots one after the other in that direction, and then there was a silence. The man must be reloading! Another flash, another explosion, but this time it was the roar of thunder and Alfie jumped to his feet and ran quickly along inside the parapet, scrambled up the roof and dived head first through the window.

Sarah was still there, shivering and dripping on the bare wooden floor of a small sparsely furnished servant's bedroom.

'Come on,' he said. He was past caring. He grabbed her hand, twisted open the handle of the door and then they were both running at full speed down the stairs.

On the landing he hesitated. Another flight of servants' stairs was in front of them, but there were sounds of voices coming from it and the noise of someone scrubbing the floor. They would not get far.

'This way,' he said, and raced over towards the ornate coloured glass window.

And he was right. As in the Montgomery household, the main staircase led down from this window, its gorgeous carpet glowing, its banisters cleaned to snowy whiteness. Large portraits of stately ladies and gentlemen stared down at the two ragged youngsters rushing by.

Suddenly the hall doorbell pinged. Alfie seized Sarah's hand and quickly pulled her behind a velvet curtain in the hallway. Now they were jammed between a door and the curtain. Alfie's heart hammered at his ribs.

'Cab ordered.' Surely that hoarse voice was familiar.

'Not by us. You've come to the wrong house, my man.' The maid's voice was pert, reminding Alfie of Nora's. 'Try next door.' And then she shut the door. Alfie could hear her footsteps going rapidly past.

Still clutching Sarah's hand, he shot out, pulled open the hall door and tumbled down the steps.

The cab driver had climbed back on to his cab seat and had raised the reins to urge the horse to go on. The lightning flashed again, illuminating his tall figure, the broken top hat with its pale green rim framing the small, turnip-shaped face. Alfie stared. Only one cab driver in London could have a hat like that.

With the strength of despair, Alfie dropped Sarah's hand, shot across the pavement and made a wild leap for the door.

'Bow Street Police Station,' he said as Sarah scrambled in after him.

'And be quick, please,' added Sarah. 'The Monmouth Street strangler is after us!'

CHAPTER 30

VICTORY!

'And Inspector Denham believed *you*?' Tom sounded sceptical. Jack gave him an uneasy glance as he leaned across Sammy and threw some more coal on to the fire. Mutsy put a paw on Alfie's knee.

'Of course he did,' said Alfie. 'I proved it to him. He sent six policemen with revolvers off in cabs and they arrested Mr Scott.'

'I think the inspector might have had suspicions,'

said Sarah quietly, 'but we brought him proof with that letter we stole.'

'It was so funny, but it was Mr Scott who called the cab. He was still waiting for it when the coppers arrived!' Alfie was laughing so much he couldn't go on.

'And our nice cabman had only just realised that he had gone to number two instead of number one when we jumped into his cab. He believed our story straight away, and he went flying down Bloomsbury and through St Giles and never stopped until he was outside Bow Street Police Station,' said Sarah excitedly.

'And when he got the policemen to Bedford Square, Mr Scott was out at the gatekeeper's lodge. He was trying to send him to get another cab, because there were no servants in the house,' explained Alfie.

'Of course when he saw our cabman arriving with policemen, he thought that was the cab he had ordered earlier that morning,' Sarah continued. 'He had begun to climb the steps into it, before he saw the policemen! The constable couldn't stop laughing when he was whispering about it to the inspector.'

'Anyway, that's enough of that,' said Alfie. 'Come on, everyone, let's go and have something to eat.'

'Did you get any money from the inspector?' asked Jack eagerly.

'Some,' said Alfie in a casual manner. He had been waiting for this moment. He picked up an old rusty beer tray and went over and placed it on Sammy's lap. 'Count us out that, Sammy, old son,' he said, trying to keep his voice steady.

And then he spilled the coins from his pocket on to the tray and watched his brother pick one up and run his finger around the rim and across the face of the coin.

'Shillings!' exclaimed Sammy.

And then he sorted them – almost as though he instantly knew how many there were – into four piles with five coins in each pile.

'Twenty!' he exclaimed. 'A whole sovereign's worth of them!'

'That's right,' grinned Alfie. In fact, the inspector had tried to give Alfie a gold sovereign, but he had preferred the rich feeling of twenty shillings. 'No worries about the rent money now,' he continued.

'The inspector says that Mr Denis Montgomery has put an extra twenty pounds on to the reward. I heard the constable whisper something about Denis being so relieved that he was not accused of the murder – "with all his debts" – that's what the constable said.' Alfie looked triumphantly at his gang and then had a quick boxing match with Mutsy to celebrate. The dog was back to his usual lively self. The cut on his head was healing beautifully.

'Tell them what the inspector said to you, Sarah,' said Alfie.

'He said that the scullery maid of the house next door to him had run away with a pastry cook,' said Sarah happily. 'Inspector Denham is going to mention my name. He thinks I will get the job. He gave me five shillings to buy myself some new clothes and a pair of shoes so that I look respectable when I go there tomorrow morning. Mind you,' she went on, 'he did say that the butler has now been arrested for stealing the silver, so I might get my job back at the Montgomery place, but I wouldn't want that even if the inspector would put in a good word for me. I'd prefer somewhere new.'

'Come on, everyone, we're going out for a meal.'
Alfie let go of Mutsy and took Sammy's arm, leading
him towards the door, and when they were all in the
street, Sammy holding on to Mutsy's collar, he
turned down Long Acre and then into Drury Lane.
The thunderstorm had moved away, the air felt fresh
and clear and the rain had washed the streets.

'Six plates of roast beef,' he said, placing two
shillings with a flourish on the counter of the beef-
house while the others sat at a table by the window.

'Six,' exclaimed the man. 'There are only five of
you.'

Alfie glanced casually over his shoulder. Mutsy had
discreetly disappeared under the table. 'Oh, the other
fellow will be along in a moment,' he said carelessly.

'Eat two yourself,' said the man with a shrug. 'I
don't care so long as I get paid.'

Jack helped to bring the plates over. The smell was
delicious. Mutsy drooled a little on to Alfie's bare
foot, but as soon as the man behind the counter
turned his back, Alfie scraped a whole plateful of beef
on the floor next to Mutsy's mouth. Two seconds
later the floor was cleaner than it had been for months

and Mutsy was sitting beside Alfie, looking every inch a well-behaved and patient dog.

Alfie returned to the counter. 'Six mugs of beer and a bowl of water for my dog.'

Mutsy was thirsty and drank the water down, but he didn't enjoy it as much as he enjoyed the beer that followed. Alfie watched him with satisfaction.

'Lady and gents,' he said, lifting his mug. 'Here's to our two heroes, Sammy and Mutsy!'

Sammy grinned in an embarrassed way and patted Mutsy.

'Take a bow, Mutsy,' said Jack and Mutsy sat on his back legs and lowered his head politely. Even the man behind the counter laughed.

And then there was a cosy silence. Outside the rain began to fall again and the evening turned dark. The lamplighter came with his ladder and lit the gas lamp on the edge of the pavement. The shop across the road switched on its lights and a wonderland of children's toys shone out through the small thick panes of glass. Inside the beef-house everything was warm and smelled good. The man came out from behind the counter, put more wood on the fire and then set a second piece of beef to roast over the flames. Alfie slipped another piece of his meat down to Mutsy and took a last swallow of his beer.

Tom belched contentedly. Sarah glared at him, but Tom just gave her a cheeky grin. He held up his mug.

'Here's to Alfie, best cop in the whole of Bow Street.'

ACKNOWLEDGEMENTS

Thanks are due to my husband who patiently
walked around the London districts of St Giles and
Bloomsbury and waited at cold street corners while I
made notes of distances and soaked up atmosphere,
to my son William who helps with computer crises,
and my daughter Ruth who is usually the first to
read any of my books.

As always, much gratitude to my agent
Peter Buckman who shares all my joys and sorrows
in this writing game and gives me the benefit
of his wisdom and experience.

Many thanks, also, to my editor Anne Clark
who has been as committed and involved as myself
in the anxieties, terrors and excitements
of Alfie and his gang.

COMING SOON

𝒯HE 𝐿ONDON 𝑀URDER 𝑀YSTERIES

THE DEADLY FIRE

The old school blazed like tinder and now the teacher is dead.

Mr James Elmore taught ragged children like Alfie to read in a crazy, rotten building on the edge of the London slums. Inspector Denham is convinced that his death is just a tragic accident. But Alfie doesn't agree. He can think of a few people who would be pleased to have Mr Elmore out of the way for good.

Was one of these the killer? Once more Alfie and his gang will risk terrible danger to bring the murderer to justice.

Available August 2010

www.piccadillypress.co.uk

☆ The latest news on forthcoming books

☆ Chapter previews

☆ Author biographies

☆ Fun quizzes

☆ Reader reviews

☆ Competitions and fab prizes

☆ Book features and cool downloads

☆ And much, much more . . .

Log on and check it out!

Piccadilly Press